"Oh, my God

Oh, my God, Kit thought again, *it's the man from the plane.* And he was none other than Joshua Parker, the man her roommates fawned over. Kit's mortification flared. She'd never expected to see him again, the man she'd shared sexual innuendo with, the man whose proposition she almost accepted. Yet here he was, and worse, he was someone famous—and the man she was supposed to interview!

"Sorry, Kit," Georgia said, "but every time I see him I can't believe a man can be that beautiful. He looks so wonderful in black. Don't you think so?"

He'd look much better somewhere else, Kit thought.

Dear Reader,

Welcome to Harlequin American Romance, where you're guaranteed upbeat and lively love stories set in the backyards, big cities and wide-open spaces of America.

Kick-starting the month is an AMERICAN BABY selection by Mollie Molay. The hero of *The Baby in the Back Seat* is one handsome single daddy who knows how to melt a woman's guarded heart! Next, bestselling author Mindy Neff is back with more stories in her immensely popular BACHELORS OF SHOTGUN RIDGE series. In *Cheyenne's Lady,* a sheriff returns home to find in his bed a pregnant woman desperate for his help. Honor demands that he offer her his name, but will he ever give his bride his heart?

In *Millionaire's Christmas Miracle,* the latest book in Mary Anne Wilson's JUST FOR KIDS miniseries, an abandoned baby brings together a sophisticated older man who's lost his faith in love and a younger woman who challenges him to take a second chance on romance and family. Finally, don't miss Michele Dunaway's *Taming the Tabloid Heiress,* in which an alluring journalist finesses an interview with an elusive millionaire who rarely does publicity. Exactly how *did* the reporter get her story?

Enjoy all four books—and don't forget to come back again in December when Judy Christenberry's *Triplet Secret Babies* launches Harlequin American Romance's continuity MAITLAND MATERNITY: TRIPLETS, QUADS & QUINTS, and Mindy Neff brings you another BACHELORS OF SHOTGUN RIDGE installment.

Wishing you happy reading,

Melissa Jeglinski
Associate Senior Editor
Harlequin American Romance

TAMING THE TABLOID HEIRESS

Michele Dunaway

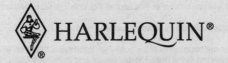

TORONTO • NEW YORK • LONDON
AMSTERDAM • PARIS • SYDNEY • HAMBURG
STOCKHOLM • ATHENS • TOKYO • MILAN • MADRID
PRAGUE • WARSAW • BUDAPEST • AUCKLAND

To Ed & the DOBC
My immortal compadres
and
To Patience & Melissa
for believing in me

ISBN 0-373-16900-0

TAMING THE TABLOID HEIRESS

Visit us at www.eHarlequin.com

Printed in U.S.A.

ABOUT THE AUTHOR

In first grade Michele Dunaway knew she wanted to be a teacher when she grew up, and by second grade she wanted to be an author. By third grade she was determined to be both. Born, raised and currently living in St. Louis, Missouri, she's traveled extensively, with the cities and places she's visited often becoming settings for her stories. Michele knows all about love at first sight—after meeting her husband on a rained-out float trip in the Missouri Ozarks, they were engaged two weeks later and married six months after that.

Michele currently fulfills both her dreams of teaching and writing, and together with her happily-ever-after husband, she raises two young daughters.

Books by Michele Dunaway

HARLEQUIN AMERICAN ROMANCE
848—A LITTLE OFFICE ROMANCE
900—TAMING THE TABLOID HEIRESS

DESTINATION: PARADISE

Don't forget to bring:

- Your clever disguise to escape those tabloid reporters.

- Plenty of money (you are an heiress, after all) to buy:
  Souvenirs for your angry father.
  A sexy bikini in the hopes that Joshua Parker will see you in it.

- Your sassy attitude.

- Your best journalistic instincts.

- Your ticket!

Chapter One

The *Tattler,* Thursday, Nov. 21
Mary Lynn's About the Town
Kit'ten Dogs Fiancé!

Only if you were there would you believe it! (See picture page one.) New York's most notorious heiress, the antic-loving Kit O'Brien, did it again. This time she upended a bowl of dog food, dumping it over Blaine Rourke, her father's favorite godson and, as speculated in this column last week, her fiancé. Sources close to the family inform me that her father, Michael O'Brien, C.E.O. of the Fortune 250 company O'Brien Publications, is absolutely furious! One has to wonder how Kit's going to pacify her father this time. Will she finally give in to his demands and tie the knot? One thing's for sure, with Kit you never know what antic she'll pull next.

"So, have you ever made love on a plane?" The words rolled silkily off his tongue, and Kit

O'Brien's green eyes widened at the audacity of the handsome male passenger who had been seated next to her for the past two hours.

"Are you propositioning me?" Although she blinked, Kit held her gaze steadfast to mask her inward shock. Despite her reputation, never before had a man been so bold, or so brash. Afternoon sunlight flickered through the first-class window as he gave her a wicked grin.

"And if I am?" His full lips curled teasingly, creating a slight dimple in his right cheek.

Kit felt shivers shoot through her body, all the way down her legs to her toes, which were cramped in what masqueraded as sensible flats. The brazen answer that teased provocatively from her mouth before she had any rational thought to stop it ignited the stuffy atmosphere. "I'd have to think about it."

"You do that and let me know." He closed his lips slowly over the edge of the plastic cup in a gesture bordering on erotic.

Ooh, he was smooth. She could lose herself in those glittering and glistening, dangerous brown eyes.

But that would be a mistake.

He turned his gaze away, releasing Kit from his hypnotic spell. Even though the possibility of caving in to his outrageous suggestion was gone, Kit felt little relief. Clamping her mouth shut, she reached forward to return her empty plastic cup to the foldout tray. Her hand shook and the cup wobbled before she righted it. Hopefully he hadn't noticed her body's immediate physical response to his provocative words.

He was quite a piece of work, she thought. They

had been talking on and off since leaving New York at 11 a.m., but right now since his attention was not on her, Kit tried to relax. Never before had she run across someone quite like him, someone who had sent her senses reeling with just one piercing look.

Whoever he was, he was temptation. A magazine lay across his lap, hiding legs clad in black jeans. A heated awareness prickled Kit's skin, her equilibrium as disturbed now as when he had taken his seat two hours ago. Then she had gazed, transfixed, until he had pointed with a well-manicured finger at the empty seat next to her.

At that moment, although she had been acutely conscious of her flushed cheeks, she could not break her stare. He had looked down his pointed, perfect Roman nose, and given her the amused knowing smile of a man used to being the center of attention. And, when he stripped off his black sport coat Kit's mouth dried to sandpaper and her throat tightened. The broadcloth button-down hinted at perfectly formed muscles. When he had moved past her to access the window seat his legs had brushed hers. Kit swore fireworks had ignited from the way her body tingled.

Kit shook from the reverie and attempted to focus. She had no time for erotic thoughts about a man she didn't know. She had four days before facing her father and his reaction to her latest public stunt. As she attempted to tug her short knit skirt down to her knees, her seatmate shifted, his black Western boots coming briefly into view. She froze.

He was a cowboy, she decided, closing her eyes

and letting herself fantasize about her seatmate. He certainly had a primitive, masculine look. Chestnut-colored hair cascaded over his collar to just above his shoulders, and Kit pictured tying his wavy tresses back with a rawhide lace.

No, she shook off that fantasy, replacing it with another. Instead she would take her fingers and tuck the strands gently up underneath a black Stetson. When she was finished with his hair, his rugged and virile hands would stroke her, yet his touch would be gentle despite being accustomed to holding fast the reins of unbroken stallions. She would trace a finger across the stubble of his jaw, and his fingers would slide lower, ready to caress her into absolute ecstasy.

Kit opened her eyes and lowered her lashes so she could venture another glance at his luminous brown eyes and heart-shaped face.

Did she really want to just slip up to the first-class lavatory with him? The illicit thought of his full lips catching hers and trailing kisses down her neck sent tremors racing down her spine. His hands would cup her buttocks, lifting her up to him, and his mouth would caress her breast. She would wind her fingers in those luscious long locks, and he would fill her body as if he were made just to please her. With knowing strokes he would take her to heights she had never imagined or experienced. Marry me, he would whisper huskily, his breath warm against her ear. Marry me....

Hold it! Mentally Kit wrenched herself from her Walter Mitty dream world and began to silently chas-tise herself. Except for his body's effect on hers, she knew nothing about him, and even if she did, she didn't do things like this! She was probably the oldest virgin in America, despite everyone's belief to the contrary. And the last thing she needed would be any more public scandal.

The now-infamous dog food incident she was running away from was bad enough. Not only was her father furious at her previous night's behavior, but she knew Blaine wasn't too happy with her, either. And she was desperate to escape both of their wraths.

Hence her editor, Eleni's, priceless expression earlier that morning. Anything had to be better than a confrontation with her father after another tabloid antic, and Kit had snatched the assignment Eleni had offered her, sight unseen and without a press packet. Who cared if she wouldn't know until tomorrow even the name of the person she was to interview? The fact that the assignment was far away from home was all that mattered. She could wait until tomorrow morning for the press kit to arrive by overnight mail. Then she would just wing it.

And she'd flaunt her success when she got back. Much to her father's chagrin she'd have interviewed whomever and written a dynamite exposé. Then her father would have to let Eleni assign Kit to more serious stories. She was tired of the marshmallow fluff her editor gave her. Wine, art and society stories had been great to cut her teeth on, but now they were boring.

Not only that, but Kit's father, the publishing icon, refused to let her write under her own name. Even with respectable stories, she had to hide behind the pseudonym Carol Jones. How uninventive. No, it was time her father gave her a real chance. Kit squared her jaw. She *would* succeed.

For a moment she wondered what the unknown person she would be interviewing looked like. If she hadn't been in such a hurry to catch her flight she might have found out. Oh, well. If it was a guy and he looked anything like the man seated next to her, well, the assignment would be a dream come true.

Succumbing to her nervous habit, she bit her bottom lip and stole another glance toward the window.

What was it about this man, anyway? Calvin Klein models couldn't hold a candle to him. With a sigh Kit rubbed her left ear to relieve the pressure, but it didn't help. Disturbed by the wicked thoughts still dancing in her head, she removed the last honey-roasted peanut from the foil pouch sitting on her tray and popped it into her mouth.

Anything to keep her mind off the way his firm fingers sensually rolled his laptop computer's track-ball as he played solitaire.

Kit settled back into the seat, her thoughts wistful. What would it be like to just once completely let go, to feel unbridled passion and get away without anyone recording her every move? Just slip up to the front lavatory with him....

Kit brushed aside the tempting but wicked thought.

Opening her eyes, she watched him move the ten of clubs before again studying his game.

"Move that eight. It plays on the nine of hearts," Kit said as she pointed out a move he had missed for two draws. "Next, move that four. It plays on that five right there."

He arched an eyebrow up expectantly at her. "Did you want a turn?"

"No."

"Just checking. I did think this game was called solitaire for a reason. But if you change your mind and want to play I'm sure we could arrange something." His dubious grin and innuendo should have infuriated her, but oddly it didn't. Kit frowned as the airplane banked slightly and the Atlantic came into her view.

"There's the ocean. We must be almost there." She pointed directly in front of his nose. Patiently he turned to her and folded the screen down. A little chill ran down her spine. The chill avalanched at his next words.

"Pity." Mirth laced his voice as the captain announced their impending approach to Miami. "It could have been so very interesting, *ma chérie. Oui?* But we now are no longer a mile high."

Kit flushed at his French-Canadian accent. Did he use that delicious accent with the women he took to his bed? She shuddered involuntarily at the illicit thought, and then she managed to get a grip on herself.

"My loss." Kit raised her shoulders and let them down slowly in an eloquent, dismissive shrug. Her strawberry-blond hair bobbed around her shoulders. "I shall have to go my whole life wondering what if…what if we had had one of those magical encounters of two ships passing in the night? What if we just missed the most dizzying lovemaking of our lives? Ah, but unfortunately life is just one big what if.''

Yes, she could pretend to be a vixen when she needed to. There was at least a sliver of truth in those mythical tabloid accounts of her sex life. She smiled to herself when he jerked his eyes away from her.

The plane began its final approach and Kit's smile faded. At the captain's orders she readjusted her seat belt, thoughts of her seatmate disappearing as the panic began. Fingers tense, she gripped the armrests. Although she had flown to all corners of the world, she still feared takeoffs and landings.

She screwed her eyes shut, missing the look of concern that crossed her seatmate's face as she began using breathing exercises in order to remain calm. Slowly she inhaled and exhaled, letting her chest rise and fall in a rhythmic motion. Few knew the fearless Kit O'Brien had an Achilles' heel. Few had seen the one-woman rebellion grip her seat as if the devil himself was flying.

In the numbing black Kit felt a stray hair lift away from her terrified face. Through her mindless panic Kit suddenly felt a fire as skin touched skin. His right hand covered her left one, his fingertips slowly caressing her whitened knuckles. An electric energy of desire liquefied her veins, sending warmth spreading through her. His touch made her forget herself, and Kit barely felt the beginning of the descent. Her body hummed from his touch, and she imagined him kissing her. He claimed her ruby lips, tasting and teasing them with his tongue until they were swollen with the blood of passion.

The blessed thump came, and brakes squealed in their whine to stop the speeding plane. Slowly Kit opened her eyes, blinking to shake off disorientation. Though she was finally on the ground, she wasn't sure she was safe. In the span of less than three hours, Kit knew her life had somehow been altered, but she wasn't sure exactly how.

Focusing on the seat back in front of her, she brought the fingers of her right hand up to touch her lips. She felt the stickiness of her lipstick and exhaled deeply. It was fantasy, although it had seemed so real.

The pressure of his fingers lifted as he abruptly withdrew his hand from hers. His voice sounded almost curt. ''We're here.''

Kit blinked twice and focused as an icy coolness descended upon her hand. Her skin still tingled, missing the heat of his fingers. ''Uh, good.''

Steadying her shaking voice, Kit continued to speak as the plane came to a stop. ''Thanks for nursing me through the landing. It was sweet.''

He raised an eyebrow and Kit wondered if he knew that her thoughts a moment ago had been anything but sweet.

''It was nothing.'' He shrugged his broad shoulders, and Kit felt her feminine ego shatter a bit as he dismissed her. She didn't know why she was expecting something from a total stranger, but somehow she did. Maybe she really was the fool her father insisted she was.

With new determination she stood, the moment the seat belt light went off. ''Well, thanks for sharing the flight. I'm off. I've got a rather difficult job ahead of me.''

"Good luck." He didn't blink, but instead looked at her as if memorizing her features.

Kit flushed. "Thanks."

He didn't respond, but instead joined her in the aisle. He towered four inches over her, and Kit stepped back. He must be at least six feet tall, she mused, watching him retrieve her two carry-on pieces with an almost practiced ease.

Oh, well, Kit thought a bit wistfully as he shrugged into his black sport coat. One more look couldn't hurt. She let her gaze travel down his shirt's button line to where it tapered to a perfectly proportioned waist. As he turned away from her, Kit decided that whoever he was, he was definitely one fit man. His masculine aura so fully commanded the small section of first class that the gray-haired woman behind her jostled her aside for a better view.

Knocked off balance, Kit crashed forward into him. He caught her easily, and under the soft cloth of his shirt taut muscles rippled. Instinctively her fingertips splayed across his firm chest. So hard, so solid…her knees wobbled as her body immediately molded to his. Delicious delirium overcame her as she inhaled his musky, all-male scent.

His strong arms steadied her. As his deep brown eyes looked down at her, Kit felt as if she were sinking into those gold-flecked pools.

"Are you okay?"

His soft-spoken words brought reality crashing

back in. Shaken, Kit stepped away, but not before she saw his eyes darken and his face cloud over.

"I'm fine," she lied, wondering if he had felt her desire. Did he know how tempted she had been by him during the flight? His guarded expression revealed nothing, and his long brown lashes hooded his eyes. Kit knew she couldn't leave it like this. This man was going to haunt her dreams, and she didn't even know his name. He at least had to have a name. Panic overwhelmed her, and she knew she had to say something to him, no matter what the consequences.

"Come on, honey. I've got to catch a connection to San Juan. Could you get a move on?"

"What?" Kit turned in disbelief to look at the woman behind her. The carry-ons Kit held crashed into one of the seats, and she paused to readjust her grip. "Sorry."

"It's okay." The woman's flat smile revealed her irritation and impatience.

Kit put on her most dazzling smile and turned around. "It was nice to have—"

The aisle ahead of her was empty. He was gone.

LESS THAN AN HOUR LATER Kit wondered what she had gotten herself into as she slid the pass card into the door handle of cabin 4648. The room certainly wasn't what she was accustomed to, or what she was expecting.

"At least it's an outside view," Kit muttered as she slowly opened the door to the last spot available on less than twenty-four hours' notice. Although the *Island Voyager* billed itself as a modern, comfortable ship, Kit decided the description didn't apply to the bottom class of cabins.

Kit wrinkled her nose as she surveyed the dorm-size rectangular room she would be sharing with a roommate. The window was directly opposite the door, and on each side of the window were two tiny twin beds. Above them upper berths, normally hidden in the ceiling, were now lowered and locked into place.

Kit faced the window. The writing desk next to her right hip doubled as a dresser. Then she turned to her left. The sink and dressing table were on this wall, along with a small closet that was next to the sink. Even the door leading to the shower and toilet was small. Not a lot of space for one person, much less two. Her bathroom at home was twice as large as the entire room.

But the cabin would have to suffice for the three nights she would be on the *Last Frontier* theme cruise.

Kit pictured Eleni's face, and now she knew why her editor had gotten that odd expression when Kit had accepted the assignment.

"I won't be able to get you a press kit or an assignment sheet until tomorrow," Eleni had said. "I'll have a package meet the ship in Nassau."

"Fine," Kit had said.

"If you're sure. They say they have one passenger spot available." Eleni had pushed a stray brown hair out of her face. "You'd have to be willing to share a cabin."

"A roommate?" Kit had blinked, but at that moment Eleni's intercom had buzzed with the announcement that Michael O'Brien was on his way up. Unwilling to face her father, Kit had said, "I'll take it."

"Get going." Eleni had waved at the door to the side hall. "You can pick up your tickets at LaGuardia. Just enjoy yourself until the information arrives tomorrow. And, Kit, be sensible!"

With that Kit had fled. And so here she was, sharing a cabin with someone she didn't know, and all of this in order to do an interview she wouldn't know anything about until tomorrow.

Kit glanced at her watch and wondered how Eleni had fared with Kit's father, the domineering patriarch of O'Brien Publications. Knowing her father's temper and his belief that his society daughter should not work, Kit was sure the morning meeting had not gone well. No, her father would be furious she had escaped to an out-of-town assignment. She grimaced. She owed her editor a big one.

Still, Kit needed these next four days. Not only would she prove herself a worthy journalist, she might even get to relax before going home. By that time, perhaps, her brother, Cameron, would have yet another new girlfriend. Her father loved the idea of getting Cameron married even more than he liked the idea of Kit marrying. Every time Cameron had a girlfriend it usually took the heat off Kit for a while.

She rotated her neck to stretch out the kinks left over from the flight. After the press packet and assignment sheet arrived tomorrow, she would do the interview, write the story, and get her father off of her back in the process.

The door opened and Kit waited for her roommate. More than one person entered, but Kit ignored the conundrum and smiled.

"Kit!" The woman Kit had had the misfortune of being seated next to on the bus from the airport screeched shrilly in delight and gave Kit a big, smothering bear hug. "I didn't believe it when I saw that you were in our cabin! I'm Georgia, remember?"

"Our cabin?" Kit blinked as Georgia released Kit and another woman stepped into the cabin.

"Right, you're rooming with me, Becca and Paula. Becca's by the pool. Paula, this is Kit, Kit, Paula. Anyway I said, Paula, I met Kit on the bus. She's really sweet and she thinks *Last Frontier* is the greatest thing since sliced bread. And since Carmen had to cancel on us, at least we've got Kit." Georgia inspected the view out the window. "Look! I can see the building where we checked in!"

"Nice to meet you, Paula." Kit offered her hand automatically to hide her shock. Oh, no. Not one, but three roommates. And they all believed she loved a television show, one she'd never even seen! Somehow she remained calm. "I'm Kit O'Brien."

"Paula Sullivan from Sandpoint, Idaho," Paula replied, returning the handshake. She assessed Kit for a moment, her direct gaze speculative. "You look familiar. Have you ever been on television?"

"Um, no," Kit said quickly, ignoring the time she had been on *Hard Copy* for chaining herself to a fence to stop an historic building from being torn down.

Paula ran a hand through the long black hair that fell to her waist and shrugged. "Probably not."

Kit shuddered with relief as Georgia bustled about the claustrophobic room like a mother hen. "I want a top bunk. Be sure to take one of the bottom bunks if you want, Kit."

"Thanks." Kit sat down on the bottom bunk opposite the bathroom as Georgia continued to open drawers and explore every inch of the tiny cabin. She hoped Georgia didn't snore. She hadn't thought to pack earplugs.

"It's 3:45! Time to get moving, y'all." Georgia remained in motion, this time heading toward the door. "I want to get registered for the events and then get a good spot to watch the boat sail. They've put all of us on late seating at 7:15. Since we'll go directly to the party afterward, everybody needs to wear their dresses to dinner. Did I tell you about the last theme cruise I went on, Paula?"

Kit ignored her roommate's conversation, her brow furrowing. She was terribly unprepared for this assignment. Normally she did tons of research, not just stuff clothes into a carry-on and wait for an assignment sheet to arrive.

"Are you ready, Kit?" Georgia was still in motion. "We sail in thirty minutes, and Paula and I want a good spot. Let's move it, y'all."

For the lack of having any better idea or plan, Kit decided to just let her roommates sweep her along. The way her luck was going, it couldn't hurt.

JOSHUA PARKER LET the warm ocean breeze flow through the brown shoulder-length locks that had less than one week until shorn short. He turned his face toward the sun, inhaling the salt-tinged air deep into his lungs. Even the fact that the boat was still docked in port, with the oily port smell mixing in, did little to discourage the feeling of well-being now filling him.

He had to admit, despite his initial reservations of participating in a theme cruise, the ship was nice, the weather wonderful. And he definitely could do without the cold dreary New York City November he had left behind. He was tired of slush melting around subway vents, tired of gray skies and tired of the gloom caused by buildings that refused to let the elusive sun touch the ground.

Even winter in Upstate New York would feel freer than the city that had snared his soul and held it captive for nine years. Escape was just around the corner, almost in sight, and Joshua wanted, with a passion, to permanently claim the open skies that hovered above his apple orchards. Even under a foot of snow his land remained unmarred by progress for miles and miles on end, glistening in its infinite whiteness.

Joshua sighed and admitted the truth—the rebel inside his soul was gone. No longer a wild child, now all he wanted was to return to the life of a gentleman farmer, as his father had phrased it many times before their big fight. It was a Jeffersonian phrase Joshua had once hated, but now it meant freedom, and freedom was what he craved.

Joshua turned from the enticing view of blue-green water that his private balcony afforded and opened the sliding glass door to reenter his suite. A blast of cool, manufactured air greeted his face, and as he sur-

veyed the sitting area of the penthouse suite, he wondered how many other people had two love seats and
a coffee table in their cabin. It was more space than
he needed. He walked over to the minibar. Since he
wasn't paying for this cruise he might as well indulge
in luxuries like three-dollar bottled water and penthouse suites.

In fact, if the cruise hadn't been so important to
the executive producers and owners of *Last Frontier,*
Joshua doubted he would have even bothered to attend. With the hit television show in its final season,
he wanted to permanently close this chapter of his
life. Sure, the fans loved the show he had created and
nurtured, but the success of *Last Frontier* had left him
oddly empty. In fact, it had burned him out and
soured him on writing.

Maybe that's why he had bought the farm, doing
four years ago what his father had first wanted for his
only son.

The age-old cliché fit best, Joshua thought. Hind-
sight was twenty-twenty. At age thirty-two he had
come full circle, finding himself in the same place he
would have been, anyway, only now he met his father
man-to-man.

The boy who had once selfishly destroyed his father's chance of a political career, not once but twice,
had disappeared. In his place was a man who knew
that parents were to be treasured, not tormented.

It was something the childish Kit O'Brien would
find out in her own time, if she ever stopped running
away long enough to grow up.

He took a long sip of the cold water and remembered the look of interest flickering behind Kit's green eyes when he boarded the plane.

Joshua grinned, recalling her expression at his proposition. The words had somehow rolled easily off his tongue, the idea of seducing New York's most notorious heiress in an airplane lavatory too irresistible to pass up.

She had almost taken him up on it, he thought with an ironic smile. She had almost consented without even knowing who he was, which had made her all the more interesting to him.

Usually people wanted something from him in return for their attentions, ever since the first *Last Frontier* convention, when he had become a fan idol. He hated it.

Worse, as much as he understood Bill Davies's reasons, he still blamed Bill for forcing him into the public light. The producer had insisted Joshua make a few cameos in the show, and he'd insisted Joshua make appearances at fan conventions.

All Joshua had wanted was to fade into the background and let only the actors' stars shine, but Bill hadn't listened to Joshua's arguments until the show had manifested into a cult phenomenon with a life of its own.

But by then the damage to Joshua's privacy could never be repaired. Now there were Web sites where people who knew nothing about him discussed his personal life and speculated on it. Stemming from that were the women who wanted Joshua Parker, the man who could possibly make them a star, not Joshua Parker, the person. Once bitten, twice shy. Been there, done that, never again.

Joshua shook his head. From her champagne-and-caviar reputation of having careened through at least three fiancés, he knew Kit probably had men pursuing her all the time.

But except for his blatant proposition made for the heck of it, he wasn't pursuing her. Nor would he want to. The price of being associated with Kit O'Brien would be too high, too public. His philosophy was to only read the tabloids, not be in them. No, long ago he'd learned the hard way to give tabloid reporters a wide berth, knowing now that they always printed the worst.

But after meeting the infamous Kit O'Brien, he'd decided she backed up all the press and rumors about her.

And the rumors said she wasn't currently available, anyway, despite last night's fiasco. The morning tabloid headlines revealed for everyone her public humiliation of Blaine Rourke, the man everyone pegged as Kit's current fiancé. Despite Kit's dumping Meaty Choice dog food over Blaine's head and down his tux at a charity dog show, "her father's favorite godson" wasn't likely to give up on getting Kit to the altar, even if one daily paper had snidely headlined the story Kit'ten Dogs Fiancé.

Although he hated the press, he had to admit he was somewhat curious as to why the society brat had done it. At the local newsstand where he normally purchased his *Times,* he had instead picked up the tabloid and skimmed the entire article. Of course the article didn't give any clues as to her motives. He had replaced the tabloid and paid for his *New York Times* newspaper.

She probably didn't have an excuse, doing it only to see her face in the papers. He'd done the same thing himself, when he was young and immature. No wonder her desperate need for escape, Joshua thought wryly as he sipped his water. Her father's wrath was bad enough that she had flown away at first light.

Still, unlike his own father, Joshua knew as well as Kit probably did that Michael O'Brien was more smoke than fire. He had tolerated Kit's well-publicized antics each time, no matter how outrageous. Joshua particularly remembered the people at the newsstand discussing her swimming with the seals in a skin-colored bikini to focus on animal rights. If he also remembered it right, there was a time she spent the night in a cardboard box in the middle of winter with some drunk ruffian to call attention to the plight of the homeless.

The grass was always greener, Joshua mused with a tinge of bitterness. Kit didn't realize how lucky she was. Time after time her father forgave her and bailed her out of her messes. He hadn't been so lucky. After costing his father his dream, his father's disappointment measured in a very long, silent period. Maybe that's why she remained so spoiled, and had been such a temptation to him on the airplane. She clearly had a passion for life.

Joshua blinked and tossed the now empty water bottle effortlessly into the wastebasket. His calves ached, so he kicked off his shoes. Here he was, on a cruise, and despite his exhaustion he was still wired. Normally he tried to catch a nap on the plane, but sitting next to Kit had made napping absolutely impossible. As he stretched out on the bed and closed his eyes, he again pictured her face as he asked her if she had ever made love on a plane. Her mouth had puckered into a surprised *O* and her green eyes had darkened to almost an emerald. Her soft reddish hair had shimmered as she shivered.

Too bad he hadn't discovered what the rest of her body felt like next to his. If it was anything like the sparks that erupted between them when she had tripped on the plane and he had caught her against his chest…loving her body would be phenomenal.

In fact, as a male who lately had chosen a long period of celibacy, he had needed to make a quick retreat from the plane in order to hide his body's immediate reaction to the feel of hers.

Joshua opened his eyes and glanced at his watch. Five minutes before he had to leave for the *Last Frontier* staff meeting. He let his thoughts drift. Kit hadn't mentioned where she was going. Miami was a connection to just about anywhere.

Not that it mattered at this point in his life. Kit O'Brien would never fit into his world. She was parties and fancy clothes. He was jeans and a cowboy hat, mud and muck and the farm near Syracuse, New York. Her limo probably took her everywhere. He always took the subway in the city.

In a little less than three weeks he would ride his horse every morning through the orchards, supervise the dairy operation and return full-time to his nonfiction writing, a career he had put on hold once he had begun scripting *Last Frontier.* She'd be deep in the party rounds of the "A" list society Christmas season.

Still, he thought with a grin as he closed his eyes and pictured the way Kit's yellow knit skirt clung to and revealed her shapely, toned legs, she was something to behold.

Chapter Two

Four hours later Kit attempted to concentrate on fig-
uring out the world of *Last Frontier*. Her roommates
hadn't sighted any of the cast members, although
they'd certainly talked about one of them, a Joshua
Parker, more than the others.

"Kit!"

Kit looked over at Georgia, who was waving a
hand in front of Kit's face. "Yes?"

"You're looking a little pale. Are you okay? Do
you need me to wrap your ankle? I brought an elastic
bandage."

"No thanks, Georgia, I'm fine. Really. I told you
it's nothing." Kit smiled reassuringly. Just her luck
to have twisted her ankle in front of a hypochondriac.

Georgia looked like a dubious mother hen. "If you
say so. If you change your mind I've got the bandage
right here in my purse. I never travel without an emer-
gency kit."

With that Georgia began watching a video on one
of the Topsider Lounge's screens. Reminding Kit of
a hotel dance club, the lounge consisted of chrome
rails and raised seating areas. The topmost seating

was upstairs on the Compass Deck, which sounded glamorous but was really just a deck surrounding the outside of the lounge.

Kit wasn't quite sure what to make of her roommates. Freely admitting to being a rabid fan of *Last Frontier,* Georgia was obviously the leader, even picking out the table on the main level.

"Here comes the waitress. What does everyone want? This round's on me." Georgia announced. Paula and Becca, Kit's other roommates, offered no resistance and ordered cocktails.

Kit shook her head in refusal, but to no avail. Georgia ordered, anyway, and the waitress moved away.

"I got you some wine." Georgia studied Kit matter-of-factly. "You only had one glass of champagne with dinner."

"Really, I usually try to have only one." In fact, it had been months since she had had more than one glass of wine, except for wine tasting, and then the procedure was to spit it out.

Kit's protest fell on deaf ears as Georgia cut her off. "You'll have one glass of wine, honey. It's good for the arteries, and it's not like you're driving anywhere, sugar. Has anyone seen either Bob or Joshua yet?" Georgia turned to search the room for her idols.

Kit smiled wryly. Again Georgia had told her how life was going to be. Georgia and her father would probably get along great, but Kit just didn't have the heart to upset Georgia the way she would her father.

The waitress returned with the drinks at the same time a cruise representative arrived on the dance floor with a microphone. Kit took a small sip of her wine, rolled it over her tongue and wrinkled her nose. Bottom-grade white zinfandel. Her father had subjected her to a wine course when she was twenty-one. While she had found the class boring, it had been the way he'd finally let her into her chosen profession. Her father didn't want her to work, and writing about wine had been her entry into magazine features.

She snapped to attention as everyone began clapping and cheering. She had missed the introduction of the man who now took the stage. Kit craned her neck and surveyed him. He was about fifty. Could this be her subject?

"Who?" She whispered at Paula's back.

"Bill Davies, the executive producer. His production company owns and distributes the show. He bought Joshua's pilot." Paula didn't even turn around.

"Oh." Kit leaned back in her chair. Frustrated that she wouldn't know until tomorrow, she studied the crowd of people who called themselves LaFrofans. Second only to Trekkies in their loyalty and devotion, Kit knew that each had shelled out at least $1,000 to come on the cruise. The room was about 60 percent women, and many of them were obviously with husbands or significant others. The participants' ages ranged from a few women Kit's age to some appearing about seventy, with the average age somewhere around late thirties to early forties.

A confused awareness suddenly caused her spine to prickle. Someone was looking at her. Kit swiveled around in her seat to look behind her, her gaze instantly connecting with that of the man from the plane.

What in the world was he doing here? He stood watching her from the doorway, the look of surprise on his face quickly masked. He didn't even have the decency to turn away. Instead he continued his obvious stare, a slight sardonic smile turning his full lips upward. Kit straightened her back when his raised eyebrows signaled his amusement, and then, after a haughty shake of her head, she turned forward again.

"What is it, Kit?" Georgia frowned. "Is anything wrong?"

"Uh, no. I just saw some guy I sat next to on the plane." Whoever the man from the plane was, she could not acknowledge him now. It was better to pretend they'd never met. She had a job to do.

"Georgia!" Paula's whisper seemed to echo, and Kit started. "Look! There! In the doorway! Look!"

Georgia turned around, as did just about everyone else in the vicinity of Paula's loud whisper.

"Oh, my God! Oh, my God! It's him!" Georgia's voice came out in a breathless rush, and Kit thought Georgia was about to have a major heart attack.

The buzz hummed loudly in the room, and Georgia began babbling about how good he looked in black, and as the room erupted into a thunder of cheers and clapping, the man from the plane strode easily into the room and joined Bill Davies on the dance floor. Fans jumped to their feet, but Kit stayed rooted to her chair, doomed.

Oh, my God, Kit mentally repeated Georgia's words, but with dread instead of enthusiasm. The man from the plane was none other than Joshua Parker, the man her roommates fawned over. Kit's mortification flared. She'd never expected to see him again, the man she'd shared sexual innuendoes with. Yet here he was, and worse, he was someone famous!

Somewhere she must have crossed a leprechaun, because she certainly didn't have the luck of her Irish ancestors.

"Sorry, Kit," Georgia said, breathlessly fanning herself with her hand. "Every time I see him I can't believe a man can be that beautiful. He's been our idol since a group of us saw him at a convention eight years ago. I just can't believe I didn't sense him—he looks so wonderful in black. Don't you think so?"

He'd look much better somewhere else. "He looks great," Kit lied with a nod, inwardly seething behind her perfect poker face. She took a long, slow swallow from her glass, letting the cheap wine burn its way like bitter medicine down her throat. She'd almost accepted this man's proposition, and worse, he knew she'd considered it.

Now here he was in front of her! Obviously comfortable in his environment of being center stage, Joshua easily answered questions and told light jokes. Kit had to give him credit, when he was with an audience he was a true performer, and they loved him.

He had changed again. This time he wore a simple black long-sleeved shirt and black weekend trousers. Both failed to hide his well-toned, lithe, six-foot body, and Kit could see why the women in the room were absolutely crazy about him. Not only had he given them their favorite television show, but he was gorgeous to boot.

Because of the lounge's lighting, auburn highlights shimmered and danced through his hair. And those lips. Those lips that had so sexily asked her if she had ever made love on a plane.

Despite her resolve to be nonchalant and impassive, Kit wanted to drop right through the floor. If she had known she was going to see him again she never would have answered him the way she had on the plane.

As if he had a sixth sense of her scrutiny, Joshua turned and looked directly at her. He saluted her with his eyes, sending his straight brows arching upward gently before they turned downward at the corner.

Kit returned his gaze of devilish delight with a haughty, dismissive stare. The corner of his mouth tilted upward in secret amusement, and Kit watched a grin rake across his face. Then he broke eye contact and whispered something to Bill Davies.

Kit took another long, slow sip of her wine. He still could be a cowboy, she thought, massaging her battered ego. He had the primal, all-male desperado look, despite his wearing dress shoes and not cowboy boots.

Kit idly fingered her now-empty wineglass. She wasn't sure how that happened, and she looked up in time to catch a small, self-satisfied smile crossing Joshua's face. For a brief moment Kit felt challenged, and she concentrated on the introductions Bill Davies was making as the *Last Frontier* actors began to cluster together on the stage.

"Fellow LaFrofans, now that you've met everyone,

we're about to get started. Tonight is simply one big happy party. Mingle with your *Last Frontier* family and enjoy the evening. We have only one request. There are over eight hundred fans on the cruise, and over five hundred in here tonight. Please, no autographs. We have a long autograph session scheduled tomorrow, and we promise you will get as many as you need then. Tonight let's just dance, drink and be decadent! Joshua?''

Joshua stopped whispering to the people Kit guessed to be the various actors and took the microphone from Bill's outstretched hand.

"Thanks, Bill." His voice was low and seductively husky. Given the collective sigh reverberating throughout the lounge, Kit figured that half the women in the room must have believed that they had died and gone to heaven. Knots formed in her shoulders as he continued.

"Tonight we've decided to start the fan cruise off on the right foot." His French-Canadian accent caused her stomach to plummet. She took a sip from the new glass of wine in front of her. Not knowing what she was up against, some liquid courage couldn't hurt.

"Each of the members of the *Last Frontier* family are going to go out into the audience like this." Joshua threaded his way past several tables and moved to stand inches from Kit. "We're each going to dance with one of the fans to start the evening. In the middle of the song, the DJ will invite the rest of you to join us on the dance floor."

Kit didn't know which was worse, the fact everyone was staring at her or the fact that Georgia was fanning herself with her hand and hyperventilating simply because Joshua Parker was standing behind Kit's chair. Kit's stomach churned, and for the first time in her life she understood fear-induced nausea.

"May I have this dance?"

Kit froze like a deer in the headlights. Despite her shock, her mouth opened. A "no" started to form but never materialized as Joshua's strong and demanding fingers closed over hers. His firm grip burned, sending waves of desire pulsating through her.

Kit pulled to free herself from his tenacious grip, but instead Paula and Georgia gave her a helpful shove that sent her right into his waiting arms. Joshua smiled and passed the microphone to a steward, who appeared from nowhere. The touch of his fingertips against her elbow felt like a flame as he led her to the dance floor.

The lights dimmed, and the first song was a soft, almost waltz-like wedding reception number. Her concentration evaporated when Joshua Parker expertly took her hands. Years of dance classes came in handy, and she moved automatically while he held her at a polite distance. Laughter and squeals of delight reached her ears as other cast members retrieved their dance partners. Kit gritted her teeth and reminded herself that she had been in trickier spots before and survived the experiences. Barely, but she'd survived.

"You did this deliberately." Kit's words sounded biting, but she made her face radiate only happiness.

"So what if I did? Imagine my surprise to see you,

ma chérie. Shocking. I never would have pictured you to be a LaFrofan. But here you are, in the flesh.''

The way he said *flesh* made Kit shudder.

''Anyway, after our brief encounter today I wanted to feel your body close to mine again.'' Joshua moved her smoothly and expertly around the floor. ''And it definitely fits mine, don't you think?''

He chuckled softly. As his deep laughter tickled her ear, Kit's nerve endings sent illicit thoughts racing to her brain. Joshua's fluid movements impressed her, as did the heat coming from his steely chest, a chest she longed to lean against. His next words brought her back to reality.

''Anyway, I've been dying to know your reaction once you discovered me onboard. Did you know on the plane that you had Joshua Parker offering to make you a member of the mile-high club? Most of the women in here would be swooning.''

He repositioned his hand slightly higher on the exposed skin of her back and pulled her closer. The simple movement of five soft fingertips shot heated tremors up and down her spine.

''I'm not most women,'' Kit returned heatedly, displaying the Irish temper she was known for. ''If this weren't a public place I would—''

''What? Dump dog food on me? Or maybe a glass of wine?''

''I don't believe you! You know who I am! You knew on the plane!''

He laughed at her outrage and twirled her, sending her away before guiding her toward him again. Kit understood his intent too late, and his twirl pressed her body directly against his. In a millisecond she felt the masculine call of every firm, tight muscle of his body and her body's own immediate weak-kneed response to it. The instant loss of sanity she had felt on the plane returned, and even the slight pain from her injured ankle vanished. She drew a quick breath as the next move pushed her away from him.

Control, Kit, she told herself. Get control of yourself. Her eyelids fluttered and she struggled to contain her body's response to the growing sensation from the simple act of Joshua's hand in contact with the bare skin on her back. She lost concentration.

"Just think, you and I meeting here, again, like this." Joshua shifted the fingertips of the hand that held Kit's, haphazardly caressing the pads on her fingers in the process. Kit shuddered. "And of course I knew who you were. Your reputation precedes you."

The jerk! Of all the comments he could have made. Kit fumed. "Well, I didn't recognize you. If I had I would have known exactly how much of a jerk you are."

Joshua laughed boldly. "I admire your spirit. Too bad we didn't take advantage of the plane." He shrugged ruefully. "But life is full of if-onlys, isn't it, Kit?"

His words trailed off as he dipped her. Kit bristled. How dare he mock her? She discovered he wasn't finished.

"You know, Kit, it's a shame. We could've had such an interesting time together. I know you want me, Kit, your body can't lie."

"*C'est la vie,*" Kit replied, using one of the few

French phrases she knew. She gave an eloquent shrug. "I'm sure I'll survive the pain. The horror."

Joshua's laughter insulted her ears. "Touché, my darling Kit. You're truly a firebrand. You've pierced my heart with your sarcasm and insensitivity for my male ego."

Only the fact she needed an interview from one of the cast members he worked with kept Kit from spiking her heel into his foot. "Somehow I can't picture you dying over it."

Joshua led her through some complicated steps with ease. "No, I doubt I will. After all, a cruise is a cruise. Still, I'm sure you'll manage to get some publicity out of it somehow. You wouldn't want Daddy to think you've turned over a new leaf. There are plenty of men onboard to dazzle."

Kit somehow checked her rising fury. The nerve of the man! The arrogance! How dare he speak to her like that. Fine, she thought. Two could play this game. She gave him a saccharine smile, and her tongue dripped syrup.

"You know, that's oh, so true. I didn't think you were the only fish in this sea."

Joshua's eyes darkened dangerously, and Kit drew herself up and raised her eyebrows at him. He shifted his fingers, his face becoming a mask. "Well said. I almost feel sorry for your fiancé. No wonder he cannot control you."

Joshua's gaze held hers until Kit looked away. Strange, foreign feelings coursed through her. What was wrong with her? One glass of wine and her guard dropped.

Kit blinked to focus. She hoped the lights blinding her were from the disco ball hanging from the ceiling and not from someone's flash. But how could someone born on Friday the thirteenth ever be lucky?

And no man had ever overwhelmed her like Joshua Parker. Over the years she had lost count of the number of men her father tried to match her with. Even good old Pete, her one and only ex-fiancé, had never moved her like this, which was why he was now happily married to someone else. Rallying her defenses, Kit readied her arsenal but the song ended.

Joshua pulled her next to him, and Kit gazed up at him, willing her features to take on a look of pure defiance.

"You were just great." His voice was husky and slightly hoarse. "I knew you'd be just great."

Kit almost didn't hear his next words, they were spoken so softly. "We'd be just great. It will be one of life's greatest disappointments that we won't get to find out."

As the length of her body pressed against his for what seemed to be an indeterminable second, Kit felt her mutinous body fully respond. Her knees undermined and weakened, she clung to him. Way too much bad wine, Kit thought, as she looked away from him, desperately trying to extinguish the fires of desire blazing in every pore.

Joshua pushed her away from him, as if somehow she had singed him too, although Kit knew that wasn't possible. He didn't look charred, in fact, he looked relieved. Clapping began all around them.

"Bravo. Again we part."

"Let's make it for good this time," Kit murmured softly under her breath. Tense from their encounter, she was barely aware of the continued clapping as Joshua guided her to the edge of the dance floor.

As he left her, Kit rubbed her elbow and tried to erase his touch. No good. She could still feel the way her wanton skin had trembled beneath his fingertips. From across the room, Kit watched as a look of sheer satisfaction and masculine amusement crossed his face. Catching her gaze, he mockingly saluted her with his bottle of mineral water. Irritated at his insolence, Kit turned away, only to face her rabid roommates, who were now descending on her for all the details of her dance-floor encounter.

Chapter Three

The long sip of cool water that slid easily down his parched throat felt good, but it did little to quench the thirst he now felt for Kit O'Brien. Joshua mentally cursed himself. He wanted privacy, not to be plastered all over tomorrow's tabloids as Kit O'Brien's newest Lothario. What had possessed him to dance with her? There was simply no excuse for his impulsive behavior. He knew better than to be attracted to a woman not his type, and he had stopped acting like a dog in heat when he was a teenager.

Worse, flashbulbs had popped during their dance, and Joshua knew several tabloids had reporters on board.

Play with fire, get burned. His father would tell him he still hadn't learned.

Rumors held that Kit O'Brien had men lined up in the wings. From her flippant attitude, something about "fish in the sea," he knew her reputation had to be true. Damn her for doing this to him. Joshua averted his gaze away from watching Kit fend off her table-mates' questions, and he willed himself to put her behind him. Just because he wanted her didn't mean anything. A realist knew he couldn't have everything he wanted, and Joshua had long ago learned to give up on wishful fantasies.

Still, his body craved how hers had pressed against his, and he shifted in discomfort. He had danced with her to erase her from his mind. Again one of his ideas backfired. He grimaced and tucked a stray strand of hair behind his ear, and stole a look at his watch. Nine-thirty. At least another hour of this farce until he could escape without incurring Bill's wrath.

"Marilyn!"

Joshua looked up to see Tatiana Terranova, the diva of *Last Frontier,* greeting a reporter with an exaggerated flourish.

"Tatiana!" Marilyn Roth from *Television Today* breezed over and took a vacant seat next to Joshua. "I'm sorry I'm late. You look ravishing. Is that a Viscountie?"

"Absolutely. You know how much I love his clothes. He makes a woman look so beautiful." Tatiana's red lips widened in a broad smile that revealed all of her teeth. For some reason Joshua had always hated Tatiana's teeth, but he didn't know why. Still, the woman who had just sat down filled him with more revulsion than Tatiana's teeth ever had.

"Hello, Joshua." Marilyn pouted. Joshua's fist clenched and he made a show of drinking from his water bottle so he couldn't speak. Even now it was hard for him to believe he had once found Marilyn pretty. Like a wolf in sheep's clothing, Marilyn had taught him that women always had ulterior motives.

They either used a man or wanted to drag out the old ball and chain and head for the closest chapel.

Marilyn's blood-red nails picked at the white tablecloth. Undaunted by Joshua's snub she continued to speak. "You're looking well, Joshua. But the years have always been kind to you, haven't they? Anyway, darling, when shall we do that interview Bill promised me? I'm looking so forward to the exclusive on your next career moves."

Joshua's head snapped up. "Surely you've got to be kidding."

He fingered his bottled water and looked for an escape. He had been young and naive when he first met her, not realizing Marilyn's true intentions until almost too late. The woman was a walking piranha, only interested in her next scoop, and there wasn't much she wouldn't do to obtain it. He turned to face the woman who had given him his first glimpse at what a nightmare the press could be.

"You're always so pleasant with me, Joshua." Marilyn didn't seem too perturbed at Joshua's comment. "I'm sure once you realize—"

His lips thinned in anger. "I'm sure Tatiana will be happy to give you any information you need about *Last Frontier*. She's starring in the spin-off, you know."

"Tatiana's not you, darling." Marilyn drew herself up and thrust her chest forward, the front of her gown gaping a little. Joshua focused on an empty glass the next table over. "Besides, Bill promised me that you would cooperate this time. This spread is important to him. He needs it to launch the spin-off. Joshua, don't you owe it to your creation?''

"Not really. I have nothing to do with the spin-off, and that's the way I want it." Joshua glanced over to where he had last seen Kit. His fingers tightened on his water bottle. He didn't see her. Had she left? Then, as some women moved past, she came into view. Joshua let his breath out slowly. Kit was holding an animated conversation with one of her table-mates and some man also standing by the table. Joshua eyed the dance floor, seeing that the other women she'd been with were dancing, quite badly he noted, to an eighties dance mix.

Joshua inhaled sharply as Kit pushed her hair back from her face. Such a simple movement, yet all of his nerve endings tingled. He watched her face. She smiled, and his chest constricted. As she laughed at something the man said, Joshua's gut tightened. He wasn't sure he liked the way the guy was looking at her. But it wasn't his problem. Kit and what she did with her life wasn't his concern.

Yet when Kit shook her head, her strawberry-blond hair danced about her chin, and his throat went dry. Air. He could do with air.

Suddenly Kit stood up, whispered something to the man, grabbed her purse and left the table. After waiting a respectable minute the man followed.

"Joshua, are you okay, darling?" Marilyn's eyes narrowed, her suspicion evident. "You haven't heard a word I said."

"I'm not your darling, Marilyn, and I never listen to what you say. Excuse me, I need to work the crowd.'' Joshua stood up just in time to see Kit heading out the exit door, the man on her heels. That woman needed a keeper. Marilyn's look of fury wasn't lost on him, but he ignored her and strode off.

KIT THREADED HER WAY through the crowd, going past the exit that led to inside hallways. She stopped in the ladies' room just long enough to convince the man that when she said good-night, she meant good-night. Upon leaving her hideout, she climbed the outside steps to the Compass Deck. A gentle breeze played havoc with her short hair, and Kit walked to one railing and looked down at the netted and empty pool. Tomorrow it would be full and active with people.

Still exploring, she turned and walked to the stern railing. From the heights of the highest deck she could see the ship's foamy wake. Kit inhaled the fresh night air teasing her face. At least today wasn't a total loss. She was at sea.

The ocean waves lapping against the shore of her parents' Long Island house were one of her earliest and favorite memories. As the midnight-blue ocean churned playfully with the boat's wake and created white foam, Kit reveled in the soothing peacefulness that reminded her of home. Night created a blanket of black and starry white, which was swallowed where it touched the horizon.

A childhood memory claimed her suddenly, and impulsively Kit looked up and focused on the first star her gaze landed on. ''Starlight, star bright, I wish I may, I wish I might, have the wish I wish tonight.'' She whispered the words aloud and then mentally added the rest. "I need to get my father off my back. I need a break."

Kit sighed and slowly exhaled. Cinderella thought a dream was a wish your heart made, but Kit had learned those didn't come true, either, despite her mother's insistence to the contrary.

As a tear slid silently down her cheek, Kit impatiently pushed it away. "Mom? Did I really tell you someday I would marry my prince?" She whispered to herself with a sad smile. How far away those days seemed, and how ironic that being at sea made her think of her childhood and home.

Her mother had loved the elegant, gilded, aged house on Long Island more than any co-op or town house, and so her father had commuted daily to the city. Ever since her mother's death three years ago the house had been shuttered, and Kit had been confined to the high-rises of New York City. She missed Summerset house and the Oyster Bay seashore.

And I miss you, Mom, she thought. A movement to her left made her start.

"Hey, you aren't planning on jumping, are you? I'm afraid I have no desire to take off my boots." The low, husky, already too-familiar voice made her shoulders tense. Broken from her reverie, Kit turned to face Joshua Parker.

A few feet to her left, he leaned against the rail with ease. In spite of herself Kit gave a short laugh.

"You aren't wearing boots."

"Ah, well maybe that's why I didn't write the screenplay to *Titanic*." He smiled, and Kit's eyes narrowed at his sudden change of attitude. "Too much icy cold water."

"Really?" She parried easily. "I would have thought it was because you didn't understand the notion of class. And, despite my having a very bad day, you won't get rid of me that easily. I've got no desire to take a swim. A jerk like you isn't worth drowning over."

"Oui." Joshua grinned and came to stand beside her. "The furious lady in the little black dress has a temper. By the way, that is a great dress. Definitely *très séduisante*. Anyway, I digress. I came up here to tell you I've been a cad, and therefore I humbly apologize."

Kit peered up at him and couldn't tell if he was serious. His brown eyes appeared as fathomless as the water churning beneath the boat. Although his gaze revealed nothing, when her eyes connected with his, a small chill of anticipation ran up and down her spine.

"What's the catch? Let me guess. You saw me crying and now you're trying to be nice. Don't bother pitying me. I don't believe it, and I don't need it."

"Ah, that one tear so angrily brushed away," Joshua mused. "Such a noble yet sad gesture. You can admit your weaknesses to me, Kit. After flying with you, I'm discovering that perhaps you hide behind that bad attitude you wear like armor. In truth, you're probably a very sensitive person beneath all those outrageous antics you do for charity."

"Excuse me? Not only do you read about me, you follow me out here to psychoanalyze me?" She drew herself up to her full five-foot-eight-inch height. "Look, Freud, go find someone else to torture with your psychobabble."

The light breeze caressed through his long, sexy hair and he clucked his tongue slightly. "Ah, good old Freud. We studied him in college, but let's not bring him into the moonlight with us, shall we?"

Kit simply rolled her eyes in exasperation. The man was impossible. First he was pushing her away, and then he was following her and teasing her in the moonlight.

"By the way, my name is Joshua." Joshua reached up and pushed his hair away from his face. "We never really did introduce ourselves."

Kit wondered if it was the wind caressing her hair that sent the quiver down her spine, or if it was the deep, meaningful look that accompanied Joshua's dare to use his name. "Look, Joshua—" Kit emphasized his name "—I'm not getting involved with you."

"Ah, she speaks my name." He grinned, ignoring her statement as he stepped towards her.

When his body invaded her space she made motion to step backward, out from under the force of his magnetism, but her feet stalled. Her body lodged itself against the deck rail, the steel oddly warming the bare skin of her back.

"After holding you close and realizing I liked it, I promised myself that you would dance with me again. Finally a lady that needs nothing from me, and I nothing from her. Only the pleasure of two consenting adults." Joshua's brown eyes glittered dangerously as he dangled the bait.

"Look, you don't know me or why I'm here."

"I know all I need to know."

The breeze raised the hairs on her bare arms, causing her to shiver. The spaghetti-strap dress that had seemed appropriate earlier now was proving otherwise. Kit rubbed her biceps. "Sorry to disappoint you. My dance card's full. Seems I have a bum foot, and one dance is all it could handle. I guess you'll just have to get yourself another girl. I'm sure someone else will oblige, you being such a big celebrity and all."

"But what if I don't want anyone else?" His voice was liquid velvet, and Kit felt it caress her like a feather. "What if I want you?"

Ooh-la-la! Her body shouted. *Control!* Her conscience shouted. It won.

"Then I guess you have a problem, don't you?"

"What about your problem? Shouldn't you give in to your own wants?"

Was she that readable? "You can go to—" She paused before she spit out the unladylike curse words. "I have principles!"

"I was beginning to wonder." A small, pleased smile teased the edges of his lips, erasing his cynical look. The result was sensual. "It's nice to hear."

"Yeah, right. You're changing your tune. Are pigs flying?" Kit's voice let him know how much she believed his statement. She shivered and rubbed her arms again.

Joshua moved even closer, and Kit's heart began to flutter. "You've intrigued me, Kit O'Brien. I want to dig beneath your surface and discover what makes you tick.''

''Now who's bringing Freud into it? What gives you the right to analyze me?'' The wind teased at the black chiffon hem, and she angrily pushed it down.

''Ah, you worry. Your hidden secrets wouldn't be for public consumption. Just mine. Every single delicious and decadent thing would remain just between us.''

Kit could have sworn his brown eyes twinkled in the moonlight. At that moment she felt the strangest longing wash over her. The power Joshua Parker held over her froze her, enticed her. All he had to do was stand near her and she lost the control she was trying so hard to keep. Her heart raced, her legs weakened and her resistance melted. Desire flowed through her, sending another chill of wanton anticipation down her spine.

''Cold? Let's get you warmed up.'' Strong fingers found her upper arms and he rubbed his palms across her skin. The friction he created did more than simply warm. At his touch Kit felt an inferno burn through her. Her body acted on its own volition. Her back arched, and her knees folded as he pulled her to him. He crushed her to his warm, broad chest, and Kit's body fused to it as if preordained to fit. He stood only four inches taller, and with her heels it was shortened to two. Her chin lifted as the last bit of her stubborn pride shattered.

''You're a dangerous man, Joshua Parker.''

Joshua's comeback failed him, and with a groan he lowered his mouth and claimed hers. The sensation of his touch sent a current through her, setting off bells of pleasure resounding in her head. His grip tightened, and he pulled her even deeper into his arms. His full lips seared hers, branding her.

"I've been wanting to do this all day," he murmured, his mouth again descending to possess hers. Kit yielded to his delightful plunder, all conscious and rationale thought fleeing at his simple caress. He pressed his tongue against her teeth, inviting himself in, and Kit's knees wobbled as her body ceded all resistance.

The call of his tongue caressing the roof of her mouth robbed her of any remaining sanity. With an ardor she didn't know she possessed, Kit responded to his kiss as she had to no other. Her arms snaked around his neck and into the long, silky locks that tantalized her fingers. Her tongue ventured forth to mate and dance with his in the ritual as old as time.

Joshua's right hand slid under her chin as he deepened their kiss, and a wanton moan escaped her as he slid his left forefinger under the spaghetti strap of her dress and playfully stroked her shoulder. Kit now understood what someone meant when she said the earth shook and the world exploded.

Fireworks detonated inside her head, and lights flashed around her as Joshua's kiss deepened even further.

"Well, well, well. I'd say you're certainly working on fan relations."

The high-pitched voice shattered the beauty of the moment, and Kit pulled away, the back of her hand automatically wiping her swollen lips.

Joshua's grip tightened on her arm, and she jerked free. One woman Kit recognized as being a cast member of *Last Frontier,* but the other woman discreetly slipping a digital camera into her cavernous bag caused Kit to worry. Press. Instinctively she knew it. Her father was going to kill her if that photo was published.

"You'll pay for this, Marilyn."

"I," Kit began, but the words escaped her so she simply snatched her purse and walked off in the direction of the stairs.

Joshua's fury knew no bounds as he watched Kit disappear down the outside stairs, her black scarf trailing like a kite. Neck muscles bulged as he checked his rage.

Marilyn gave Joshua a wry smile as she lit up a cigarette and handed the lighter to Tatiana. "I just needed a smoke and the sun deck is just a little too popular. I mean, it's just out the Topsider's doors. And, of course, you know how fans follow Tatiana everywhere."

Marilyn exhaled slowly and deliberately as she sized up Joshua. "Besides, Bill's been looking for you." With absolutely no concern or fear of Joshua's anger at her intrusion, Marilyn flipped cigarette ashes over the rail.

"I told him that last I knew you were working the room. I would say that you were working it pretty fast. Looking for a better offer? Well, she's an easy little thing."

Joshua refused to dignify Marilyn with an answer. Defending Kit would be unwise. Anything he said to

Marilyn would be twisted to her advantage. He shoved two fists into his pants pockets and scowled as Marilyn inhaled again.

As she blew out another stream of smoke, Joshua gazed at her mouth for a moment, wondering how she could pollute it. Then again, she always polluted something. The front-page trash she'd written about Joshua under her pseudonym Mary Lynn had cost his father his dream, but Marilyn didn't care who she hurt. She had called Joshua a simpleton, laughed at his fury and moved on to her next victim.

He glared at Marilyn and Tatiana as they blocked his path, inwardly raging at them for destroying the kiss of a lifetime. Kit's kiss had been fresh, tantalizing. He had explored her mouth with abandon, finding the mixture of wine and honey so delicious he had lost control. Never had he tasted such sweetness.

Ire and revulsion filled Joshua, at himself for degrading Kit, and at Marilyn for having the gall to make snide comments. He watched Marilyn flip the cigarette butt over the railing despite the signs posted indicating otherwise.

"You know, I might be wrong, but there's something really familiar about your—" Marilyn deliberately searched for a delicate word "—companion. What did you say her name was?"

Joshua's irritation reached a crescendo. He refused to confirm Marilyn's fishing expedition. He'd wasted enough time. He needed to find Kit.

"I don't think she wanted to be introduced to you. She's got class." Joshua purposely ignored Marilyn's next tasteless comment as he pushed past her and headed for the stairs that led down to the club. Still he had heard her comment and it burned in his ears.

"That's all right, darling. I'm well aware of who Kit O'Brien is. You're right, she is classy. So classy she always rates the front page. See you in the papers."

Joshua's eyes blazed in fury as he threw open the door to the brightly lit interior passageway. With a final curse he set off after Kit.

ONCE IN HER ROOM, Kit threw her purse down on the neatly turned-down bed and sat down with an agitated thump. The mint carefully placed by the cabin steward on her pillow went flying. What was she thinking? What had she been doing? Two black shoes hit the floor and slid under the bed as she reached up under the black dress and hooked her fingers into her pantyhose. Kit removed the silky sheers and sent them flying under the bed with a vicious kick. Standing again, Kit assessed the damage to her face in the mirror over the sink.

Her lips looked as if they had been thoroughly kissed. Wait, who was she trying to fool? They *had* been thoroughly kissed. Her knees still wobbled from the way his mouth felt. She gently touched her puffy lips, remembering the way his lips had pressed down, possessing her. She closed her eyes for a moment, recalling how his tongue had searched her entire mouth, claiming it for himself. Kit's eyelids flew open, and she stared at the reflection of her eyes in the mirror. Makeup remover. She needed makeup remover. Kit turned and found her toiletries case and brought it to the sink. With almost robotic movements she began to cleanse her face.

"Kit?" Kit heard Georgia's voice as the door to the cabin opened a crack.

"I'm in here," Kit called, splashing cool water on her face to remove the last of the soap.

Georgia stepped into the room. "Are you okay? Everyone's headed to the theater, and I was worried about you. You never returned. Is it your ankle? Do I need to wrap it for you?"

"I'm just really tired. I've had only a few hours of sleep lately, and I've just hit my wall." A small, tight smile accompanied her little white lie.

Georgia nodded sagely. "I understand, sugar. Eventually the body just drops."

"Exactly." Kit nodded. "So don't worry about me. I'll be asleep when you get back. Enjoy the show and the buffet. You can tell me all about it tomorrow."

"You're sure you don't want to go?"

"No, go and have a great time." Kit reassured Georgia again and reached for her dental floss. "Honestly, I'm fine."

"Okay." Georgia reached for the door handle. "You know, I can't believe how good Joshua Parker looked tonight! I know you think I'm crazy to like the writer better than the actors, but, ooh, sugar, in most cases the fantasies are better than the reality, y'know? But not with Joshua Parker. The reality is definitely much better. Wouldn't you agree? Anyway, they're showing the two-part series finale in the theater tonight, so, if you're sure you don't want to go…'' Georgia's voice trailed off, her desire to leave evident. Kit gave Georgia a resigned smile.

"Good night, Georgia. I'm sure I don't want to go. I'll catch the shows when they finally air on TV.'' Kit wrapped the floss around her fingers. As the door clicked, Kit faced herself in the mirror again. A half smile teased at her cheek. She didn't have any fantasies where Joshua Parker was concerned. But the reality… Kit's green eyes suddenly tormented her from the mirror.

He had ravaged her with just one kiss, a kiss she had been powerless to stop. Fireworks had exploded in her brain, sending her catapulting out of control. Wine, sea air, a starry sky, and Kit had been putty in his hands. Joshua Parker had possessed her with just a kiss. Where was her New York City aloofness and disdain? Such a foreign feeling—no one had ever evoked the level of passion that Joshua drew from Kit in one dynamic kiss. In fact, she had dumped dog food over Blaine for a lesser sin—announcing their engagement—which was why she was hiding on the cruise in the first place.

Makeup removed and teeth brushed, Kit slipped out of the black dress and dropped it into a heap on top of her bunk. Frustrated, she flipped on the television set. The ship was running *Last Frontier* reruns non-stop, and she sat down to watch an episode. Kit didn't understand the premise of the show, that man had conquered dimensional space and time travel, yet man had still not bettered his primeval ways. Throw in a couple of aliens and outer planetary beings, and the whole show somehow came together into a fast-paced, special-effects wonderland that had quickly become a cult sci-fi classic.

Kit turned off the television set. All she had learned was that the drifters were a group of people who wandered through time and other dimensions doing good deeds until their lives expired, whatever that meant. She still didn't know which actor she was interviewing, either. Kit stared around the cabin and turned on the TV again. For a moment she thought she saw Joshua in a Hitchcock-like cameo.

He was wearing black, and the color suited him, giving him the sleekness of a panther. Watching his body move for just the few seconds he was on screen only heightened her awareness of how his body had felt under her touch. With a resigned shudder Kit turned off the TV and glanced at her watch. It was just now eleven, and Kit knew that all the LaFrofans were in the theater one deck below watching the screening of the last two episodes.

Like a caged tiger Kit paced the room in her silken pajamas, too on edge to sleep. Finally she yanked off her pajamas and, with a determined fierceness, dressed in a pair of flowing black pants, a white silk top and a matching black jacket.

She was not going to hide in her cabin. She was Kit O'Brien, by God, and she had weathered much worse unsavory press than being caught kissing someone. She pushed the thought of her father's reaction out of her head. She could deal with him later. Compared to Joshua Parker and the illicit thoughts she had of him, her father would probably be the easier of the two. With newfound determination to get Joshua Parker out of her head, Kit slipped her feet into plain black skimmers, ran a brush through her hair, grabbed her purse and headed toward the casino.

Chapter Four

Earlier the casino had been dark and empty, but now it hummed with life. While the casino was nowhere as large as the casinos she had experienced in Las Vegas, Nice or Monte Carlo, Kit immediately liked the intimate atmosphere.

Despite being two decks high, the casino was cozy. Steps led to an upper level, but Kit decided to remain where most of the gaming tables were. She surveyed the lower level room for a moment before heading over to the cashier to purchase some chips.

"Give me twenty red chips." Kit watched as the girl swiped the credit card for $100, counted Kit's chips out onto a tray and shoved both through the hole. Kit took the tray expertly and headed for the blackjack table with the red placard she had chosen upon her arrival.

She slid into the second open spot near the left edge of the semicircular table, and gave the young dealer a warm smile as she placed her tray on the table. The dealer was playing against three other players.

"Good evening," he greeted her, and Kit guessed he was about twenty-three. "Are you in?"

"I'm in." Kit slid a five-dollar chip onto the table. She gazed at her three tablemates. If the rings on their fingers were an indication, they were married. It was a perfect situation, even though with no one to her left she would be playing the blackjack position of third base. "How's everyone doing tonight?"

"Breaking even." The man to her right laughed, his slightly double chin bobbing as he slid some chips forward. "I've been sitting here with Connor for a while now, right, Connor?"

Kit gave Connor an amused smile. Like all casino workers, Connor was wearing the typical white oxford shirt and the standard black dealer's vest. As she looked him over she decided he would do for a harmless flirtation. Of course, the casino dealer didn't compare to Joshua, but forgetting Joshua was why she was here. She brushed the thought of Joshua's lips out of her head and gave Connor another smile.

"Holding the late shift, Connor?"

"Yes. I'll be here until we close." He gave her a grin.

Time to begin. After Blaine and Joshua, she needed something harmless, something she could control. She lowered her lashes. "Well, I won't be here that long, if you take all my money."

"I'm sure you're a winner." Connor gave her a grin to emphasize his words.

Success. Kit gave him a wide smile and mentally congratulated herself for having pegged his character from across the room.

Unlike Joshua, Connor would be nothing but harmless banter. After her father that morning and Joshua rattling her senses, Connor was exactly what she needed to massage her trashed ego. This situation she could control. She turned as a waitress approached.

"Absolut vodka with a lime." Kit threw away her last restraint and handed the waitress the ship's credit card. "I've had nothing but bad wine tonight."

"Terrible," Connor agreed. "It can sour the mouth for better things."

He was definitely smooth, Kit decided. She slid three chips forward as her bet.

The waitress came back, and Kit took a long swallow of the clear liquid. She knew that Connor was watching, waiting for her. "I'm good."

"I'd say you are." Connor's tone was low as Kit won. "Luck's with you. How's that drink?"

"It's doing the trick." Kit laughed as the vodka warmed her throat.

"Been a hard day, has it?" Connor gave her a cheeky grin, and Kit ignored the fact that his smile didn't melt her like Joshua's. She was not going to think of Joshua. Especially not the way his kiss had made her insides melt.

"This trip has been anything but what I thought it would be." Kit twirled her swizzle stick before she took another long swallow. Putting the drink down, she slid another five-dollar chip forward as her entry into the game. "Be good to me, Connor."

"I try to never disappoint a lady." This time he gave her a cheeky grin.

Kit wasn't sure how long she sat there, but as she finished her drink and ordered another, she realized it hadn't helped. Joshua was still as much present as if he were sitting next to her. Somehow she had to get him out of her mind.

Kit looked at her cards. She had twenty-one, and she turned over her cards. "I'm impressed. I'm usually so unlucky."

"Maybe it's time for your luck to change." Connor's eyes held hers as he slid the chips over, his fingers brushing her hand lightly as he did so. Unlike Joshua's fingers, the sensation left Kit flat.

Kit lowered her voice conspiratorially. "Perhaps my luck is changing."

But obviously it hadn't. The seat that had remained vacant all evening suddenly found a body.

"Where's the dress?" The low, husky voice seared her ears, and every hair on Kit's neck sizzled to attention.

Kit wanted to bury her face in her hands. "Left behind with a host of other bad memories."

She slid a chip forward and refused to face the man whose knee was now dangerously touching hers. She tried focusing on the game, but he leaned toward her.

"I've been looking for you," Joshua whispered so that only she could hear. "I've been walking the ship for an hour."

Kit's voice was cold. "I didn't want to be found. Especially by you."

She scowled. When had her glass become empty? Connor slid a playing card in front of her. Kit stared at it. She couldn't even focus. "Connor, I'm calling it a night. Are you working tomorrow?"

"I'm teaching poker lessons at three and then I'm going over to Paradise Island."

"Paradise Island?" Kit stacked her chips on her tray.

"The casinos are there. I take it you've never been to Nassau."

"No. But obviously you have."

Kit gave him a warm, teasing smile as she stood to leave the table. Just one last little flirtation, Kit thought. Might as well. Joshua thought she was a tart, anyway. Let's see how he liked being right.

"Enjoy the rest of your night, Connor. Maybe I'll see you in Paradise."

Connor shook his head and grinned. "For you I'll be there. But if you can't find me, call me at 5689, and I'll show you Nassau instead. The view from the water tower's fantastic." He gave her a cheeky smile and turned back to the people now taking seats.

"I may take you up on both." Kit gave him a parting smile and walked toward the cashier to cash out. "I came out ahead," she announced to the girl who couldn't care less.

When the clerk's eyes widened in obvious appreciation, Kit realized she had been followed.

She felt him approach her and inwardly groaned. Her mind silently cursed him, and she crossed her arms across her chest in a gesture that was needed more to hide her body's instinctive arousal than to be a sign of displeasure. Kit reached for her credit card and shoved it in her pants pocket. She turned to look at Joshua. By his body language she could tell he was angry. Probably at her. Well, that was tough, Kit thought. He'd pushed enough of her buttons; turnabout was fair play.

"Now what do you want?"

"We're taking a walk," he said simply. He gripped her elbow firmly and led her from the casino. They stepped out into the bright hallway, and Kit blinked a few times. The lights seemed somehow brighter than before, and she felt a bit dizzy. The sharpness of his voice assaulted her ears.

"What was that all about?"

"What was what all about?" Kit echoed, her voice cracking as she tried to feign innocence. She pulled on Joshua's arm to slow him down. Now that she was walking, she knew she was a lot less sober than she had previously thought.

"Your little comments." Joshua spun her around to face him. His eyes held no amusement, and Kit inhaled deeply, sensing every bit of his animal magnetism. Whatever cologne he was wearing, Kit hated to admit, smelled good. Very good. And to think she had almost escaped. Her body lurched forward slightly, and he righted her and pushed her back.

"Oh." Kit's mouth dropped open into a mischievous grin. "I told him I'd see him in my dreams."

WHEN KIT ANNOUNCED that she would be dreaming about the casino dealer, Joshua's whole body shook with a sense of controlled fury that was fast becoming a habit around Kit O'Brien. She was lucky he didn't throw her overboard so she could truly experience all the fish in the sea.

Maybe that would stop Kit from reverting to any more tabloid antics. And he had mistaken her for having principles. The thought irritated him to no end.

Couldn't this woman see why she brought on all her own tabloid misery? She would learn about the photo Marilyn had taken of Kit at the blackjack table in tomorrow's tabloid. "Speaking of Marilyn, there she is again. Come on."

With a tighter grip this time, he grabbed her elbow and led her through the hallway. He brutally stabbed the elevator button with his forefinger.

"Hey! Where are you taking me?"

"Not where I'd like to." Poised like a panther, he guided her soundly into the elevator. He jabbed the button for the A-deck, and the doors slid ominously closed. Only then did he unleash his pent-up fury. "I spend an hour looking all over this blasted ship for you, and when I finally find you you're drunk and picking up the blackjack dealer."

"I'm not drunk, and I wasn't picking him up!" Kit's voice sounded slurred and she wobbled a little. "Why? Are you jealous?"

"Whatever for?" he parried, irritated at himself. Yes, she definitely needed a keeper.

"I don't know. Maybe because you want me."

When she swayed toward him, he caught her and crushed her against his chest. That was a mistake. A wave of desire rippled through his body, and when her lips parted slightly, it was all he could do to concentrate.

Kit's drunken invitation was obvious, and it took all his mettle to refuse it. Instead he waited her out. When she realized the kiss wasn't forthcoming, she forced herself to step back out of his arms and defend herself some more.

"Oh well." She shrugged.

Joshua frowned but kept quiet. If he didn't get her back to her cabin, he would be in deep trouble.

"Did you know I was on a roll? I won about fifty dollars. It's illegal to control these games, you know? I was just flirting. I never flirt. It's my life, why can't I flirt if I feel like it? It made me feel better. I deserve to feel better. I've had a terrible day. I'm stuck in a too-small cabin with three people I don't know because it was the only spot available. I'm hiding out from my father, but my picture's about to be all over the tabloids tomorrow, so he'll know not only where I was but that I was kissing you!"

"You just don't get it, do you?" Joshua loomed over her and peered down into her eyes, which were now a smoky emerald.

"Get what? That you're a jerk?" Kit insulted him with an angry slur. Whatever had been in her glass had not only loosened her up to flirt, but it had also loosened up her tongue with abandon.

"I mean, why are you even here? Haven't you done enough damage? My father will kill me when he sees the picture tomorrow. You've made me look like a fool, Joshua!"

Joshua wondered if the elevator could move any slower as Kit slurred out his name. The only one who was making Kit look like a fool was herself. And he'd been there, done that himself. Maybe this was his penance, why he felt the need to save her. Maybe it was the fact that he found her intriguing. He didn't want to know.

"Look," Kit started in again. "I may not know

about *Last Frontier* but I know all about you. I'm sick to death of hearing my roommates rave about you! I know from personal experience that your type isn't worth it.''

''What makes you think you're my type? You're a city girl. I'm a country boy. Why would I want you?''

''You just do.''

Because her chin thrust forward daring him to contradict her, he couldn't resist baiting her. Her face was flushed, the result enticing. ''No, Kit, you want *me*.''

''Oh, to hell with you, Joshua Parker! Right now I just want to be as far away from you as possible.''

''Really.'' Joshua clenched his teeth. His frustration threshold had been breached. ''You're lying, Kit. Tell me that again after this.''

Before Kit could even attempt to move, he swept down upon her and captured her mouth with his own. Her arms came up to push him back, but her resistance was futile and short-lived. He deepened the kiss, determined to send whatever thoughts she may have had in her head scrambling. Her body was completely under his control. He could feel it respond, telling him yes, this was what she wanted. As she leaned against him, tilting her head back, he took her mouth.

He knew too much alcohol had inebriated her, but the feelings she aroused in him were fresh, invigorating and more passionate than any he had ever experienced before, and he didn't want them to stop. Joshua felt his own control slip as her lips ran over his, her tongue tasting his mouth as if she were a dying woman finding water.

Her arms snaked up around his shoulders as her

knees weakened, and Joshua groaned as she pressed against his own evident arousal. In spite of all their differences, he wanted her. It was that simple. Her hands slid up into his hair, fisting his long, silky locks, and a shudder reverberated through him.

"Joshua." She moaned his name softly, and without a second thought Joshua pulled her lips to his again.

An abrupt ding snapped him back to reality. What was he doing? With a muted groan he pushed her out of his embrace. Like a moth to a flame, he thought wryly. He was going to get burned. Kit's murky green eyes opened, shock evident as she tried to focus on the open elevator door.

Joshua put his hand out so the door wouldn't close as she backed hastily away from him. Kit O'Brien had another weakness besides flying, and he had found it. Him. Despite whatever she'd had to drink, her responses to him were not alcohol induced.

No, there was another fire in Kit O'Brien besides her temper, and despite his reservations about their differences, it was as essential as breathing that he explore it. But not right now. Right now she needed sleep. Still, unable to help himself as he took in her reaction to his kiss, he gave her a self-satisfied smile. "Enjoy those dreams, Kit."

He stepped back inside the elevator and watched the retort fade on her lips.

OUTSIDE THE ELEVATOR Kit watched the door close. She turned and wobbled the thirty feet to her cabin. Damn him. Who did he think he was? For a moment

Kit thought of defying him and going somewhere else, but when she saw two—or was it three?—images of her cabin door she changed her mind.

Her roommates hadn't returned yet, and for the second time Kit brushed her teeth and slid into her pajamas. She drew the covers up to her chin and stared at the wooden bottom of the bunk above. She could still feel his lips, his fingertips and his strong chest. She had wanted him. Needed him even, and she never needed anything. She had always made sure of that. He had been tempting her all day, and Kit rolled over and furiously pounded her fists into her pillow to relieve the tension she felt. It didn't help. She put her head on the pillow and tried to close her eyes. The darkness was even worse, for now the only image she could see was Joshua's face as he leaned to kiss her.

Chapter Five

Mary Lynn's About the Town
Kit'ten Plays with Other Men!

Kit O'Brien definitely lives up to the old adage that there are other fish in the sea. Less than twenty-four hours after dumping dog food all over her fiancé, Blaine Rourke, Kit was photographed passionately kissing Joshua Parker, writer for the hit sci-fi show *Last Frontier*. (See photos page one.) Not only were they dancing and clinging to each other, but Joshua even rescued Kit from the casino dealer she was shamelessly flirting with. (See photo page 1.) Is this the reason Kit dumped (literally with dog food!) Blaine at the charity dog show yesterday? Has she replaced him with Joshua, or is this just one last fling before Kit settles down and gets married? Hmmm…I wonder what her father thinks of this?

"Eleni!" Michael O'Brien strode forcefully into the *Scene* editor's office without warning. With a flick of his wrist the tabloid hit her desk, knocked over her pens and almost spilled her coffee. Intent on getting some straight answers, Michael didn't give it a second thought. "Eleni! I'm assuming you have an explanation for this?"

"Uh?" Eleni was clearly at loss as she read the tabloid article.

Michael's eyes narrowed as he sat down with a thump in one of the leather wing chairs. "Please tell me this isn't happening to me."

"It's not happening to you," Eleni offered.

Michael threw up his hands in exasperation. "If it were anyone but you…" Michael's voice trailed off.

"I know, I know. I'd be fired," Eleni finished for him. "So, since it's me, what do you want?"

Michael leaned forward. He'd known Eleni and her husband for more than twenty years. When Charles had died the O'Briens had comforted Eleni, just like Eleni had comforted him when his wife had died. Besides that, he trusted her, which was why she was Kit's editor. He hadn't wanted his daughter to be a journalist, much less work at all. He had a son for that.

"What I want is for her to marry Blaine, settle down and have babies. I don't want her plastered over the tabloids kissing some strange man and being branded as trying to pick up another."

"Oh, Michael. I know you want Kit to settle down. But you can't arrange a marriage for her," Eleni chided gently. "She's rebellious. She wants you to accept her for who she is, not for what you want her to be."

"Nonsense," Michael scoffed. "Kit needs molding. She's too spoiled. It's time someone reined her in. I never should have allowed her to work here in the first place. It's given her ideas. She needs protection, not freedom. I'm her father. I know what's best. As it is I practically had to blackball her so she couldn't get another job in this town."

"Michael." Eleni gave him that look of hers, but Michael refused to respond to it. Eleni sighed. "What are you proposing? She's on a cruise ship. You can't just fly down and haul her off from the middle of the ocean. She's actually on an assignment."

"That I don't believe. What's she writing on, cheap cruise food? That'll be a widely read feature." Sarcasm evident, Michael frowned.

Eleni seemed to hesitate. "Actually she's supposed to be interviewing the man she was, uh, getting to know."

Michael jumped to his feet, an act that left him wheezing a little. "Oh, great. Just what she needed. It's bad enough she has to write at all."

Michael held up his hand to stop Eleni's protest. "No Eleni, don't defend her. Not this time. I know you're like a second mother to her. But as of right now I'm overriding her assignment. It's over. Canceled. Even if she goes ahead, I won't print it. Not even under the name of Carol Jones. Now, she needs to stop this nonsense and get back here. Blaine told me this morning he'd still have her. She'll accept his proposal when she gets home, and that'll put this tabloid nonsense to rest. Until then I'm going to call her and tell her exactly what I think of her actions."

Eleni looked at him, shrugged and said nothing. Michael frowned. He did know what was best for his wayward daughter, right?

SOMEONE HAD OPENED the curtains. Bright sunlight poured into the room, and Kit rolled over and buried her face into the pillow.

"Oh, good, you're up," Georgia said brightly as she bustled noisily about the cabin. "I thought maybe you were going to sleep all day."

"No, not me." Kit tried to sit up. Blood rushed to her forehead like someone banging on a door, and she eased back down and covered her eyes with her hand. "I just have a headache, that's all."

"Well, two Tylenol and some fresh air will cure that." Georgia maneuvered around the cabin with an energy that hurt Kit's head even more. "Becca and Paula are already at the Voyager Café for brunch. We're pretty late, so rise and shine."

Kit dragged herself to a sitting position and stared at the clock. Eight-forty was not late. She was on vacation, wasn't she? Well, at least until the press packet arrived.

Sighing, she rubbed her fingers in a circular motion around her temples and shrugged off the last bits of sleep. Her hangover wasn't terrible, just excruciating. What had made her choose vodka, anyway? Champagne, wine and then vodka. For someone who avoided more than one drink, what had she been thinking? Come to think of it, ever since she'd been on the plane she hadn't been thinking correctly.

Shuddering, Kit looked at Georgia. Already

dressed, Georgia was wearing plaid walking shorts and a white crewneck, short-sleeved sweater. There would be no rest for the weary. "What's the schedule for today?"

"We're all attending the question-and-answer forum at ten, and I knew you didn't want to miss that. During our free time this afternoon a bunch of us paid to go on the ship's tour of Nassau. Then there's the meet and greet with the cast at five-thirty. From that we're free until dinnertime. Tonight is the costume party. Are you going into Nassau?"

"You know, I didn't buy any tour tickets." Kit reached for the glass of water and the pain relievers Georgia was handing her. "The travel map said most everything is close to downtown, so I'll probably spend some time wandering Nassau. It's one place I've never been." Kit swallowed the tablets. She couldn't remember Connor's extension, not that she would ever have called him.

Georgia peered at her, watching Kit as if making sure she took the medication. Georgia replaced the glass on the sink. "How extensively have you traveled?"

Kit reached down, a feat that made her feel as if ten drummers were practicing inside her head, and grabbed her bag. She pulled out the small black United States Passport. "This is my third one, and it's almost full." Kit tossed it to Georgia, who pounced on it, first looking at Kit's personal identification and then thumbing through stamps of foreign countries. Georgia handed it back to Kit. For once Georgia was speechless.

"Did the ship's daily itinerary arrive?" Kit rose slowly out of bed and gingerly waited for her head to stop thumping.

"It's on the table there." Kit followed Georgia's point. "The ship has done a great job of working around the *Last Frontier* events."

Kit scanned the oversize piece of paper and the prepaid tours and decided that she could do just as well on her own with the *Fodor's* guide she had purchased at the airport.

Moving slowly over to the window, Kit looked out. She was surprised to see another cruise ship just across the water and then one farther, behind it. Wide pedestrian and car paths were evident between the ships, meaning the *Island Voyager* was docked at Prince George Wharf. Therefore Rawson Square and the Ministry of Tourism were only a short walk away.

"You signed up for a tour?" Kit's head continued to pound as she dug through her suitcase, finally pulling out a pair of red shorts and a white cotton sleeveless T-shirt.

"Yes," Georgia said, fiddling with an itinerary sheet. "We didn't want to go to the beach knowing that we'll be on the private island all day tomorrow. Instead we'll see Fort Charlotte, Fincastle and the Queen's Staircase, Fort Montagu, and we get to go in the Junkanoo Museum, and I think the Pompeii Museum. We have to be at the purser's desk sharply at noon or they'll leave without us. Oh, and we get to peek at Atlantis, as well."

"You'll have a great time," Kit said.

"We hope so. Oh, before I forget, you got a package. Let's see. I put it right here.'' Georgia bustled for a moment before passing Kit an overnight express envelope.

"Thanks.'' Kit pulled the flap and pulled out some of the contents.

"Wow!'' Georgia breathed. "If you don't want that picture, can I have it? He is so gorgeous! You are so lucky!''

Kit held the eight-by-ten glossy photograph, seeing with horror the image she never hoped to see again.

Joshua Parker was her interview subject.

Fingers shaking she shoved the picture back in the envelope and buried the package in her suitcase. "Look, I'm up. Give me fifteen minutes and I'll be ready for breakfast.''

"And then the Q and A,'' Georgia reminded her.

There was no way Kit wanted to face Joshua. Not now. She had to gather her thoughts, figure out how to regroup and solve the mess she was in. "I may skip that and head into the straw market. You can tell me about it later.''

Kit didn't hear Georgia's response as she turned the shower on full blast and shut the door to the bathroom. The hot water felt good as it ran down her back. Kit squeezed a quarter-size amount of shampoo into her hand and began to massage it through her hair. He was her interview subject. Somewhere the Fates were laughing at her, because the memory of Joshua Parker would not leave her alone. How did he know where her cabin was, anyway? He had told her he had been looking for her.

For what? Hadn't he already done enough? Their

picture was probably plastered all over the tabloids today. Her father would not only know where she was, but what she was doing and with whom! And, if Kit knew her father, he would pull the story from her, especially when Eleni told him she was kissing her subject.

How to salvage this disaster? She needed this story to prove herself. If it was good enough, her father wouldn't turn down printing it no matter what he threatened. After all, he was a businessman at heart. Therefore she would make sure her story was fantastic, if not even better. Kit raised her chin, letting warm water stream down her back. Somehow she would succeed, even though she knew from Georgia's comments that Joshua hated the press and never gave interviews.

Kit finished rinsing her hair and continued to mentally process the shreds of last night. Joshua Parker had kissed her. Twice. Kit involuntarily put a finger to her lips before reaching for the soap. Her body had never reacted like that before. Certainly Kit had experienced longing before, but never to the extreme heights of wanton passion that Joshua sparked with only a kiss. Joshua. Reluctantly Kit turned the water off and reached for a towel. She dried off, dressed and wrapped the towel around her head. Stifling a yawn, she stepped out into the room.

He was sitting on her bed. In the mirror she could see the disbelief, shock and embarrassment that all crossed her face at the same time. Her mouth was even open. Realizing she had been had, she clamped her mouth shut.

"Joshua got tired of waiting," Georgia said, the lie obvious. She smiled. "So he dropped in to make sure we were on our way."

"I can see that." Kit bit her lip, too astonished to say anything else. She stared at Joshua. Because the room was too small to have a chair, he was reclining with ease on her unmade bed. He was dressed in khaki shorts and a dark-blue shirt, and his brown hair fell easily away from his face to his shoulders. He certainly looked as though he had slept well.

"Good morning, Kit. Everyone was wondering when you were going to wake up. How's your head?" Joshua took a moment to freely appraise her, and she bristled as he ran his gaze over her long legs. With audacity he even ran his gaze all the way down to her bare feet, making Kit very aware that her toenails were free of polish.

Kit gave Georgia an incredulous look of disbelief. "You've already been out," she accused loudly.

"Of course," Georgia said, her feathers unruffled. "I told you that. You mumbled something, but you probably slept through it as you did all of our showers. Paula and I got up and watched the sunrise. It is the most gorgeous day out there. Sun, surf. And, anyway, I would have told you last night that we were meeting Joshua for breakfast but you were sound asleep when we got in at one." Georgia looked at Joshua. "She didn't even stir."

"That I'd believe." Joshua grinned at Georgia. "She was pretty tired."

Set up. Of all the luck, Kit wanted to pull her hair out. Hair. Oh, my God! She was still wearing a big white towel on her head. Her face reddened and she reached up and yanked the towel off. With her fingers she combed out her strawberry-blond mane, creating a tousled mess. She grabbed for the brush and began to straighten it out, very much aware that Joshua studied her every move.

"I need to blow-dry my hair," Kit said lamely, his steady stare disconcerting her.

"Well, we've waited this long," Georgia quipped. "Finish up."

Joshua's brown eyes tormented her as she grabbed the hair dryer. Within two minutes her hair was finished and she gave it a quick spray.

"I'm ready," Kit announced, moving toward Joshua. She gestured to the suitcase under the bunk. "I just need some shoes."

Joshua shifted his muscular legs over slightly but refused to budge. Only two inches from him, Kit squatted down to retrieve socks and her brown walking shoes. Skin brushed skin, and a shock quivered through her. Needing to escape his touch, she leaned forward to grab the socks. Instead she lost her footing and fell over backward, landing on her rump. Slightly discombobulated, she simply put her socks and shoes on, stood back up and followed Georgia out the door without saying a word.

Joshua fell in step beside her, his long legs easily matching her stride as they followed Georgia to the elevator. "You look good without makeup," he said. "I noticed that last night."

"I'm glad I have your approval," she testily began,

but a hand on her arm stopped her. Joshua pulled her to a complete stop, and he turned her to face him.

"It's a new day." His brown-eyed gaze bore into hers, like a prospector striking gold. "Let's start it off right. No planes, no dances, no casinos."

Kit gazed at him, wondering if he was going to kiss her. Her lips parted slightly, but even though his lips pursed, he did not move forward. Instead he spoke again.

"No sarcasm, no snide comments."

She opened her mouth to respond, but his expression silenced her. Thoughts of kissing him vanished.

"That goes for both of us, Kit. Let's see if we can actually have some time together where we get along. It's another day. Shall we begin anew?"

"Are you two coming?" Georgia called from around the corner. "I'm tired of holding this elevator door and I'm hungry!"

"Agreed?" Joshua's expression was deadly serious, and Kit trembled.

She had no idea why he was pursuing spending time with her. It didn't make sense, but what other choice did she have? No matter how her body responded, she had to interview this man. Her future depended on it. Somehow she had to find the right time to ask him.

"Agreed." Kit nodded once. "I can do that," she mumbled, too shocked at her wanton desire to kiss him again to come up with anything else.

"Good." Joshua visibly relaxed. His left hand came up under Kit's right arm and he guided her to the elevator.

"I like this elevator," Georgia said as the doors opened on the sun deck. "So convenient. Right by our room, although I guess we could have walked inside to the solarium and up. But this way— Hey, look! The pools are filled!"

As Joshua and Kit shared an amused glance at each other, Kit felt a flicker of hope. He would let her interview him, she decided, it was just a matter of timing.

Becca and Paula had saved seats at a table for five just outside the doors to the Voyager Café.

"Finally," Paula greeted Kit. The table sat directly in the warm, tropical sun and Paula lifted up her sunglasses to peer at Kit. "We've been wondering if you got lost."

"No, I just slept in. Sleep is a rarity in New York." Kit stood at her chair and wished she had thought to wear her sunglasses. Joshua had already put his on, and the effect was totally sexy but disconcerting. She couldn't see his eyes, the only clue to what he was thinking.

"Well, Paula and I couldn't wait so we've gotten our food already. Food is inside there." Becca pointed to the doors that led to the Voyager Café.

"Come on." Joshua said.

Kit followed him through the buffet line and filled her plate with grapes, a blueberry muffin and a waffle.

"That's it?" Joshua asked as he loaded up some pancakes on the plate that he had already covered with sausages, muffins, eggs and fruit. "You barely have any food."

"I'm also not on my exercise routine," she replied,

grabbing a glass of orange juice and balancing the plate.

When Joshua waited for some sliced ham, she left him at the buffet table and returned to her seat. Kit placed her plate down. From her vantage point she could see Joshua stop to talk to a fan as he worked his way out from under the awning.

"You owe me the rest of the story later, Kit," Georgia whispered conspiratorially. "Joshua tracked me down before the showing last night. He wanted to apologize to you or something like that, and I was the last person he'd seen you with. Anyway, once I got my jaw off the floor, I told him we were roommates. And, you know how I am—I couldn't tell him no, so I took him to our stateroom. Anyway, you weren't there."

Kit popped a grape into her mouth. Chewing and swallowing gave her a moment to mull over what Georgia had said.

"So where were you? After you weren't in the cabin he took off after you."

"I was playing blackjack." Kit frowned as she continued to contemplate what Georgia had revealed. Joshua had been hunting her down? It didn't make sense.

"It's just all so crazy." Kit cut her blueberry muffin. "He found me in the casino playing blackjack and escorted me back to my cabin."

"Blackjack?" From across the table Paula raised her dark-brown eyebrows in speculation as she jumped into the conversation. "You were at the casino? Georgia said you were going to bed."

"After she left I couldn't sleep so I went out for a bit," Kit replied.

"I see." Paula waited for more, as did Georgia.

"I was playing at the table of a very cute dealer," Kit confessed. "I won about fifty dollars, and then Joshua escorted me back to my cabin."

Paula watched as Joshua threaded his way through the tables. She nodded to herself wisely. "That explains it. At the midnight buffet he insisted on meeting us for breakfast. Georgia, of course, agreed immediately."

"I mean, can you believe it?" Georgia gushed. "Joshua Parker talking to me. Me! You do understand, right?"

"Of course." Feeling disconcerted, Kit shredded the muffin pieces and put a tiny bite in her mouth.

So that's where Joshua had gone after she had gone to her cabin. Scheming with her roommates and making sure she didn't contact Connor. Oddly the thought pleased her. "How long was he at the buffet?"

"Just long enough to cook up this scheme," Paula replied. "Beware, Georgia's got you married to him already."

"I do not!" Georgia shrieked in mock indignation.

Kit practically spit out her muffin. "Right! Like there's a fat chance of that. My father has been trying for years. His latest attempt involves his favorite godson, a kid who used to pull my hair and put tree frogs down my shirt. No offense, Georgia, but I'm certainly not going to let a woman I just met do me in."

"Oh, no offense taken, sugar," Georgia said. "But you must know that I've got three successful matches under my belt. There was my cousin Beth, and then—''

Kit interrupted her. ''Look, I think he figures that when he's with me he's safe from all the women hitting on him.''

''Uh-huh. I'm sure that's it.'' Georgia forked some leftover scrambled eggs into her mouth and quieted as Joshua approached.

''How is it?'' Joshua asked as he slid into the seat next to Kit and began unrolling his silverware.

''Fine,'' Kit replied. Just his nearness affected her. Her food suddenly tasted like sand.

The rest of breakfast seemed dried up as Kit hardly spoke while Joshua, Georgia, Paula, and Becca carried on like old friends.

''The Q and A starts in fifteen minutes.'' Georgia suddenly announced.

''Becca and I will go save some seats.'' Paula stood up. ''Georgia, finish your food.''

Georgia turned to Joshua. ''When do you need to get there?''

He rolled his eyes in amusement. ''Here's how it normally goes. Bill is already there making sure everything is set up. Everyone else except for Tatiana will arrive on time. She'll be fashionably late by at least five to seven minutes. That gives me plenty of time to finish eating and get there without looking too bad and inciting Bill's wrath.''

''We need to catch the tour by noon.'' Georgia glanced at Joshua. ''Kit didn't sign up for any tours. She's got a *Fodor's* book instead.''

''Ah, so you're an expert.'' Joshua's expression reflected only genuine interest. "Well, you must indulge me, then. I'm not on any tour, either, and I want to see Old Nassau while I'm here."

Kit shifted uncomfortably. "Are you suggesting we see the town together?"

"What a great idea!" Georgia interrupted, a beaming smile on her face. "Kit, you've got to go. You two could rent a scooter or you can always get a surrey. I wish *we* would get one of those cute horse-drawn carriages, but we're going on a bus. I had enough of buses yesterday." Without missing a beat she turned to Joshua. "Did you know that Kit's on her third passport and that it's almost full? You should ask her about some of the places she's been while you're out."

"Really, Georgia." Kit's protest fell on deaf ears.

"Besides, it'll be a great way for you two to begin getting to know each other, don't you think, Kit?" Georgia smiled sweetly at Kit.

Bushwhacked and set up again before 10:00 a.m. Afraid of her response, Kit ate the last of her muffin to save herself from answering.

"Exactly." The voice came from Joshua, and Kit looked at him in surprise. He was now busy planning her day with Georgia.

"That way I can take her to lunch." The wink he gave Kit made her stomach flip.

"Somewhere authentic," Georgia advised. "None of those chain places you find all over the world. I'm always telling my husband, he's a pilot, you know…"

Kit tuned Georgia out and took a sip of her orange juice. Her heart dropped down to her feet as she stole a glance at the man who was taking over command of her day. Animatedly he and Georgia were going over details and checking them twice, and Kit simply gave up. This cruise was not going to be about escaping from her father and getting better assignments. It wasn't even going to be relaxing. No, it was going to be about *Last Frontier* and Joshua Parker, and there was nothing Kit could do about it.

But, the idea didn't necessarily sound all that bad. An excited thought wiggled its way into Kit's brain. She was spending all day with Joshua Parker. She could start covertly interviewing him during the day, and Kit could already picture the story on the cover of *Scene*.

The idea filled her with revulsion.

She choked on her juice.

"Are you okay?" Joshua looked over, concern evident.

"Fine," Kit mumbled into her napkin, grateful when he turned his attention back to Georgia. Kit never had material that warranted the front cover of the magazine, much less even her own name, but an exclusive on Joshua Parker was definitely cover material. It would prove her merit to her father.

But the thought of invading Joshua's privacy like that without his knowledge bothered her. Kit sighed. She didn't like the catch-22 she had gotten herself into. Deep in her heart she wasn't spending time with him for the story. She had to admit she was attracted to him. Her need to spend time with him was for her own greedy self.

Chapter Six

"Hey, stop trying to escape." Joshua slid up next to Kit when the question-and-answer session ended. People milling around suddenly realized Joshua was in the audience.

"Scratch that, escape sounds good." He gripped her elbow and guided her back toward the stage. "This way." He led her quickly up the steps to the upper level and out the door to the Showtime Deck's solarium.

"Alone at last." Joshua turned to her and grinned. Below them they could see people lining up at the shore excursion desk. They walked down the corridor past the shops. "Now I can ask you all those personal questions like how'd you sleep?"

Kit colored slightly. His conversation was too intimate. "My head pounded unmercifully until I got in the shower, and I didn't make it to paradise," she answered. "If that's what you're after."

Joshua gave a deep, throaty laugh. "No dreams? Even about me? What a pity." His sympathy was in jest, and Kit knew it. "I suppose I'll have to be the only thing you see all day," he said, seeing her bemused expression. "Except for the sights of Nassau, of course."

"Of course." Kit's heart jumped a little. "You know, I have to admit I was wrong about you. I'd pegged you for a cowboy of some sort, riding the range in Texas or Montana."

"Close," Joshua said, guiding her through the photo gallery. "I grew up on a farm near Quebec. We had cows, horses, chickens and pigs. I grew up wanting to compete in the rodeo." He saw her dubious look and chuckled. "Yes, they have those in Canada. I also played hockey like everyone else, but my father forced me to quit after I broke my arm. I still love the country, and I bought a farm in the Finger Lakes region a year ago. The house is being rehabbed right now. Here's our exit."

After scanning their cruise ship cards through the machine to record their departure, Kit and Joshua left the ship at the B-deck forward exit. The warmth of Nassau instantly enveloped them. They bypassed the taxicabs and instead walked the length of the wharf using the pedestrian walkway built down the middle.

The overall wharf was designed like teeth on a comb, and when they reached the end of their walkway they turned right, onto the main pedestrian thoroughfare, and continued toward town. Underneath one of the covered areas of the walkway a Bahamian band played, and at the end of the walkway someone pressed a free shopping map of the city into her hand. Someone else asked her if she wanted to rent a scooter, and Kit shook her head and opened the map.

Priding herself on her ability to walk and read at

the same time, she jumped when Joshua reached out and pulled her toward him. Her body crushed against his, and a sudden infusion of heat flowed through her.

"They drive on the other side of the road here," he said, pointing out a cab beeping at them to get out of the way.

"Thanks." Kit acknowledged as he guided them safely off the roadway. Her body still tingled from his touch, and to cover it she lowered the map and scanned the area. Duty-free liquor stores touted their wares, men gestured for customers to line up for a surrey or a scooter, and endless tourists with shopping bags pushed past on all sides. Awareness of Joshua prickled Kit's skin, and she started walking forward to regain control.

"Slow down, speedy, and let's decide what to do first. It seems like everything is around here." Joshua reached out and pulled Kit to a gentle stop. Releasing her he motioned at all the people milling about with video cameras. "What do you want?"

What she wanted was to be safe in her cabin, far away from the dilemma she faced in getting to know Joshua Parker. She shivered, glad she'd hidden her eyes behind her shades.

"Shops, museums, it's up to you, Kit. We're at Bay Street, which, according to your map, is a duty-free shopping mecca with upscale shops. We could start a walking tour here."

She debated. "I don't know. Duty-free is nice, but I can get this stuff anytime on Fifth Avenue, even if I have to pay taxes. She paused when she saw a sign.

"I certainly don't need to get my hair braided. When I travel I like to see the sights."

"Me, too," Joshua replied as they crossed Bay Street and walked up to the House of Assembly. "Georgia said you're well traveled."

"Boy, Georgia told you a lot, didn't she?"

"She definitely likes to talk."

That was for sure. To avoid answering, Kit instead chose to look at the two-story pinkish buildings with the white columns. She quickened her step so she could read the inscription on the statue of Queen Victoria, which simply told the queen's name and dates.

"So you like to travel?"

"I love it." He glanced over at her, and Kit could see the intricate pattern the sun's reflection made on his sunglasses. "Last summer I took five weeks and backpacked my way across Europe. It was one of the best adventures of my life."

Lucky guy. "My parents refused to let me do that. I got the standard 'Paris experience' instead. I stayed with a family friend for a summer, and it was boring. I never did run away with some guy named Pierre, despite press reports to the contrary."

"The oh-so-truthful press."

"Most of it about me is so far-fetched. Next they'll have me giving birth to an alien."

"That's why I stay away from it and refuse to give interviews. I don't need any alien babies."

Kit laughed despite the frustration she suddenly felt. He didn't give interviews, and she needed one. Now what? "So, will you be traveling this summer?"

"No. It's time to go home." Joshua's tone flattened.

Kit studied him with interest, trying to read something in his profile. Maybe this was something she could use in her story. She brushed that thought aside. More intriguing to her was the fact that Joshua seemed somehow different from the night before, yet the powerful aura surrounding him still existed. This version of Joshua's personality didn't make Kit nervous. Rather, she found herself enjoying his conversation, especially now that it was becoming more personal. She pushed the guilty thought that she was using him out of her head. "Where's home?"

"After I left Quebec I grew up in Upstate New York near Canandaigua." The English pronunciation of the Native American word rolled off his tongue with ease. "The land around there is relatively flat, but it's in the Finger Lakes region and it's beautiful. Mom settled there because it was a day's drive from my father's house. When she remarried we moved to Albany."

Kit shot him a quizzical look. "They're divorced?"

"Yeah. Since I was ten. I've got dual citizenship because of it. Dad's French-Canadian, Mom's American."

"Oh. Brothers and sisters?"

"Two half brothers from my mom's second marriage and two older sisters from her marriage to my father. All of my siblings either live in New York or Canada. None of us got very far from home. You?"

"I didn't get far from home, either. I still live there, although I have my own floor of the apartment. Other than that, I have one brother, Cameron. He's four years older and unmarried. I guess that makes him your age. He's too much of a playboy to settle down for at least another year or two.''

Intent on looking at the changing scenery, Kit missed the odd look that crossed Joshua's face as he guided her around a corner. She realized they had made a loop back to where they had started. This time Joshua guided her toward a horse-drawn carriage.

''Our surrey awaits,'' he said.

The native driver smiled at her, and he helped Kit up and onto the seat of the open-air surrey. The surrey's small size forced Kit to press close to Joshua. The top was up, providing shade, and the gray dappled horse and the driver began the tour of the buildings with Parliament Square, which was across from Rawson Square.

Kit sighed as the horse plodded past the pink colonnaded complex of government buildings that sat literally on a square of bricks. ''Such pretty buildings. British tropics.''

''If you say so. We weren't seeing anything, and I was worried about your ankle. Georgia gave me the health lecture while you were in the shower.'' Joshua put his hand on top of hers, and a tingle shot through her. As the new sensations caressed through her, she knew that her ankle was the least of her worries.

''So what made you choose writing and producing?''

''Actually, you could say we're kindred spirits, Kit.'' Joshua frowned. ''I had a weak moment during college. My friends tell me I was doing all sorts of improvisations. I'll be honest. I don't remember a thing about what I did. Anyway, I wasn't applying myself to my studies and my father was furious. I'd embarrassed the family. He had great hopes for me to make something of myself. After all, I'm his only son.''

"But you are a somebody. Millions of fans love the show you created."

Joshua laughed hollowly. "That's not enough for my father. He considers himself a gentleman. There are certain occupations that one just does not do."

Kit didn't know what to say to that. Joshua's plight sounded so familiar to her own. Maybe they were kindred spirits. Because of that, she also knew that if she'd told someone this stuff she wouldn't want it revealed. That thought bothered her, and she shuffled a little in her seat as Joshua continued.

"Anyway, I started writing and sold pieces here and there. My big break was when Bill Davies bought my concept for *Last Frontier* about nine years ago. So here I am." He looked around him suddenly. "Speaking of where I am, where are we?"

Kit leaned back against the worn leather seat of the surrey. "We're wherever you paid him to take us."

"We aren't seeing much of Nassau."

"You know, that's okay."

Behind her sunglasses Kit closed her eyes. Her brain processed the information Joshua had just told her. There was more to the story, of that she was certain. Joshua had glossed over it too fast. It was almost imperceptible, but not to Kit. No, her talents were being wasted on marshmallow-fluff stories. She could read people, and she could get fantastic material for stories. If only her father would let her.

Kit bit her lip and frowned. Somehow Joshua's life had divided him from his father. That sounded familiar, almost too close for comfort. Her own father never understood her. If he did, she wouldn't be in this predicament, trying to figure out what exactly was the right thing to do.

Time to find a safer topic, one that didn't hit so close to home. She opened her eyes and turned to face him. "Have we decided where we are going?"

"Queen's Staircase," the driver announced suddenly. "Must walk steps to fort. Take footpath down from top. Meet you there." The driver's accent made his fort sound like fart and Kit giggled as Joshua shot her an embarrassed glance begging her to shut up.

Kit and Joshua slid out of the surrey. "I don't notice any other surreys around."

"I paid him extra to whisk us away," Joshua explained. "He might be breaking the law."

"Great. That'll be a good headline. O'Brien and Parker arrested on way to rendezvous." Kit turned her face to the warm sun. She had to admit, she didn't care.

A tour guide greeted them at the top, and after tipping him for his rapidly spoken lecture, they rounded the white water tower and walked up the road.

When they reached the fort, Kit gave a pleased, low whistle. "Impressive for something built to guard against invaders who never came."

Joshua reached for Kit's hand. "Shall we tour it?"

"Will our driver wait?"

Joshua laughed and toyed with her fingers. The motion sent waves of desire running through Kit. ''I paid him extra and told him that I'd give him another bonus when we're done. He'll be at the bottom of the hill. Trust me.''

Strangely she did, and that scared her. Hesitantly she reached out and took the hand Joshua offered. ''Lead the way.''

As JOSHUA WALKED TOWARD Fort Fincastle with Kit, he couldn't care less that the small fort was built by Lord Dunmore in 1793. He didn't even care that the three cannons that guarded the hillside were now rusted. No, what he cared about was simply enjoying his day with the vivacious Kit O'Brien.

She had a childlike exuberance, worth millions if it could be bottled and sold. Despite her hangover, Kit explored with abandon. She wanted to see it all, do it all. He could now understand why she pulled some of the stunts she did. It was impulse, an innate drive to feel everything, do everything, be everything. She grasped life's brass ring unconsciously, knowing that if she fell, Daddy would always love her and take her home.

She didn't know how lucky she was, Joshua thought, watching her feel the stone wall, her fingertips rubbing the texture as if memorizing it. His own father had never been so generous, even when Joshua had begged for forgiveness.

After Kit surveyed the main, cannon level, he followed her up another set of stairs. She had taken over, and he let her show him the triangular roof covering part of the fort. From the top they had a good view of the white water tower and the shoreline.

"There are the ships." Kit pointed toward the horizon where the *Island Voyager* and several other cruise ships were docked. "You know, I should have brought a camera. The view is phenomenal."

"I'm sure you can get one at a vendor booth. Come on, I want to check something out."

Kit gave him a quizzical smile. "What?"

"You'll see." He smiled, leading her back down to the cannon level. It was time he did something impulsive himself. "Come here."

He opened one of the doors set into the stone wall. The small stone room was lit only by outside light that would trickle through the iron bars on the door. He helped Kit down the one-foot drop and pulled the door closed. Now he had her where he wanted her.

"Jail, I guess," he teased, reaching for her arm. Her skin prickled from the lack of the sun's warmth. Or was it from his close proximity? He wasn't sure.

"Maybe it was ammo storage," Kit added.

"It's cooler in here." Joshua's voice was husky.

"What are you doing?" Her voice held a quaver of anticipation. Did she want his touch as much as he wanted hers?

"Killing two birds with one stone."

"What?" In the shadows her reddish hair seemed to shimmer in the faint light.

"Our secret rendezvous and being arrested. Or kissing you where no one can see. No cameras." He pulled her toward him until she was pressed against his chest.

"Oh," Kit began, but his descending mouth cut off her next words. Perhaps he should yield to impulses more often, he thought, as Kit's passion flared. She opened like a flower for him, and he deepened his kiss.

Kissing Kit O'Brien was becoming a drug that he couldn't get enough of. When she dug her fingers into his shoulders, he didn't care if her life was too public for him. His tongue explored parts of her mouth that he didn't know could be so sensitive. Wow.

At the sound of footsteps and voices Joshua quickly drew back away from her. The last thing they needed was to be photographed again. But he couldn't let her go. Not yet. "I'm not sure what's happening here between us, but I want to explore it more."

The arrival of a tour guide saved her from a reply.

The door opened and another couple came in.

"Harry, I want a picture of me behind bars," the woman said.

The man adjusted his Nikon lens. "Sure, Enid."

"That's our cue," Joshua whispered in Kit's ear. And probably not a moment too soon, he thought. He wanted her. The kiss had proved one thing: she also wanted him. He was grateful the darkness hid his conflicting emotions. He needed to protect himself, yet he wanted her. He wanted to bed this woman. The force of it hit him. Given her wealthy city background he knew she wouldn't understand him or his goals, but she would accept him into her bed until he left. Yes, definitely time to get out of the dark before he succumbed and kissed her again.

As the tour guide began his speech, Joshua pulled Kit around Enid and toward the door.

"We'll be sure to thank Lord Dunmore that he built this expensive fort for the raiders that never came," Joshua told the tour guide. "It looks like a paddlewheel, from the sky."

"You're right," the guide replied with enthusiasm. "It's designed in that shape. You can tell from the water tower—"

Joshua heard Kit stifle a giggle. Good. At least he'd gotten a response out of her.

"We're heading there next." Joshua led her out the fort.

"You were terrible, baiting that tour guide." Kit laughed, and Joshua didn't think he'd seen a more beautiful sight than Kit laughing. It lit up her whole face.

"Terrible," Joshua agreed, the seriousness he'd felt earlier evaporating. Laughing with her, he pulled her along the path to the water tower.

KIT COULDN'T BELIEVE the fun she was having. When she'd learned that morning Joshua was her interview subject, the bottom had seemed to fall out. Now she just didn't care. After thinking it over, she wasn't going to worry about setting up a formal interview with Joshua. She'd just write down her observations. That way he wouldn't know, and she wouldn't ever have to tell him. Plus, she wasn't using him, she wanted to get to know him. It really was that simple, she rationalized.

Therefore, she found herself smiling at all the merchants lining the pathway, although she declined their offers of three T-shirts for ten dollars, gospel cassette tapes and straw hats. She paused for a minute by the one-use cameras, but when Joshua tugged on her arm and motioned to the historical marker she had to go read that.

"Stairs or elevator?" The woman inside the tower said as Joshua paid the admission fee.

"Elevator," Joshua and Kit said at the same time. They laughed and the woman opened the metal gate to the elevator. Unlike the smooth elevators Kit was accustomed to, this one moved slowly, and she gripped Joshua's hand. He gave her an odd look, but squeezed her hand tight. Kit relaxed, feeling safe from just his touch.

The rickety elevator ride was worth it. After a few more steps, Kit and Joshua took in the 360-degree view from the top of the white tower. From their vantage point they saw the poorer sections of town, the paddle-wheel shape of the fort, the ships, the deep azure water and the bridge to Paradise Island and Atlantis.

"I'm glad you shared this with me," Joshua said suddenly. Kit's heart fluttered. What was it about this man? She'd hardly known him twenty-four hours, and already he had reduced her to a quivering mess of emotions. Despite the warm sun, Kit shivered as the cloud of her ultimate goal suddenly overshadowed her.

"So, was that reporter planning on interviewing you?"

"Who, Marilyn?" Joshua snorted. "Absolutely

not. I'm on vacation, and I'm done with interviews. Finished. Never again.''

"Oh." Not good, she didn't add, as she followed Joshua back inside.

As he predicted, their driver was waiting for them on Sands Road. When the surrey next stopped it was for lunch.

"Our driver says this restaurant has the best food around. I told him if it turns out to be true he'll get an even better tip than I promised."

"I am hungry," Kit admitted. "Must be the tropical air."

"Of course, that must be it." Joshua raised his eyebrow and taunted her playfully. Kit flushed, glad he didn't directly mention her earlier hangover or their kiss.

The surrey driver reached up a gloved hand and helped Kit down.

"Come." The driver grinned. "You eat."

Kit and Joshua followed him inside, and as soon as the hostess greeted him, their surrey driver disappeared into the back of the restaurant.

The hostess seated them at a table for two away from the rest of the late-lunch crowd. Kit wiggled down into the brown woven chair that fanned out behind her like a cobra, encompassing not only her back but also her head.

"So, we're in an authentic Bahamian restaurant. What are you ordering?" Joshua asked.

"Authentic food of course. I promised Georgia, remember? Besides, I've traveled the world, and you'd be amazed at what I've tried. Snails, ants, various kinds of beetles, even dog.'' She grinned as he wrinkled his nose in disgust. ''Just kidding about dog. I've never been to South Korea or Vietnam.''

Joshua shook his head as if repulsed. ''Okay, just checking.''

Kit's green eyes mocked him. ''Why, are you chicken?''

''No, but chicken sounds good.'' Joshua scanned the menu as the waitress brought the canned soft drinks they had ordered.

''Ha!'' Kit snatched his menu from his hands. ''I'll order for us, and you'll eat it. Be an adventurer. You're on vacation.''

''As long as it's not a vacation my stomach would want to forget.'' Joshua grimaced, and succumbed.

He had to admit, she'd chosen well. Kit ordered the house specialties: okra soup, baked crab and conch salad. The automatic accompaniment was johnnycake, a Bahamian bread. Despite Joshua's initial reservations, he wasn't about to be outdone by the bold and fearless Kit O'Brien. He had to admit lunch was excellent, both for the food and the company.

Kit was unlike any woman he had met before. Poised yet not stodgy. Innocent and fresh. Joshua found himself unable to tear his gaze away from her when she smiled. Little laugh lines formed around her green eyes, and almost invisible dimples crept into her cheeks. He had to admit that while Kit wasn't the most beautiful woman he'd ever been out with, she was the most natural. Even without makeup she was radiant. As she savored her ice cream, he let his eyes rove over her, his manhood quickening as he did so.

There was no doubt about it, he wanted to make love to her. Maybe then he could get her out of his blood. And he needed to get her out from under his skin. She'd infected him with her tinkling laugh and playful pout. But she was not the woman for him. He knew that.

They were like fire and ice, totally incompatible. While she was tormenting her father, he was rebuilding the bridge to his. She lived in the fast lane; he wanted the dirt road to nowhere. He wanted peace and quiet; she wanted press and notoriety.

No, he and Kit O'Brien could never be anything but a temporary diversion, some temporary pleasure. And even then he'd have to count on her being discreet, something she'd proven over and over in the tabloids that she wasn't.

No, she would never understand the rift he had had with his father. After tearing his father's political life to shreds and tossing the man's love aside like trash, Joshua knew he had to complete this last act of reconciliation. He owed this last debt to the man whose dream he'd destroyed.

From Kit's latest tabloid actions, it was apparent she didn't recognize when she was wrong. Therefore she needed to just be a temporary diversion, some little cruise magic to be enjoyed before time ran out. He would teach her some lessons in discretion before the ship docked Sunday.

His eyes followed the smooth curve of her shirt's neckline, his eyes resting on the rounded mounds of her breasts that were hidden from direct view. Just the thought of reaching for them, touching them, removing her shirt and kissing them was enough to drive him mad. Loving her body would be phenomenal.

"Are you okay?" Concern emanated from Kit's voice, and hearing it brought Joshua back to reality. None too soon, he thought wryly.

"No, I'm fine," he responded smoothly, reaching up to run a hand through his hair. "Why?"

"You were staring at me."

"Why not? You're beautiful," Joshua said.

Kit's face flushed and she put her spoon down. "Are you done eating? We still haven't seen the straw market yet."

"No, we haven't." Joshua gestured for the bill. While he paid it Kit looked at her fingernails. From her movements he knew she was aware of his desire. He had never known anyone like her, and she was under his skin. He wasn't comfortable with the sensations she evoked in him, but he had to explore them.

And he knew she wanted him. No, a temporary romance couldn't hurt. Not if he played his cards right. He helped her back into the surrey, and as they sat down their legs touched.

The movement sent electric shocks of desire through him, and not one to waste an opportunity, Joshua brought his lips down upon hers. The kiss ricocheted through his entire being, and as if it was possible to melt further in the hot Bahamian air, he did.

She jerked away from him, her arms pressing him back as his lips nuzzled forward, searching for more. "We're almost there, I'm sure," she whispered as she tried to find her voice.

"I just want to take you to a nice quiet spot on the ship—" Joshua slid his finger down her neck and Kit shook uncontrollably "—and kiss you all over."

WHAT WAS IT ABOUT THIS MAN? Kit flushed a flaming scarlet as the driver gave her a cheeky, knowing grin and urged the horse to a walk. As the wheels click-clacked over the bricks, she pulled out her sunglasses and hid behind them. No man had ever spoken to her with the absolute directness of Joshua Parker, and she'd shot down anyone coming remotely close.

Unlike her tabloid reputation, Kit had zero experience with men. The few kisses she had participated in certainly hadn't rocked her to her knees like Joshua's did. His kisses made her want to lose control, to stop at the nearest hotel and get lost in crisp white sheets. She found herself wanting to run her hands under his shirt and across his chest. Kit shook her head in disbelief. She sounded lascivious, lustful. So unlike herself.

She gazed at him. Could Joshua be such a skilled lover he could draw this reaction from any woman? True, woman lusted after him because he was gorgeous. She didn't have to look past Georgia, Becca and Paula for confirmation on that count. Bewildered, Kit shifted in her seat.

"Straw market." The surrey driver's voice ripped through her turbulent thoughts as he reached his hand to help her down. The break was welcome; she hadn't even noticed the surrey had stopped.

"We'll walk back from here. This has been great."

Joshua reached for his wallet, and Kit's eyes widened at the number of bills he handed the driver.

Kit took a moment to gather her thoughts by continuing to walk. Joshua had to run to catch up. "Hey, wait! I thought you didn't want to shop."

"I want to look at everything," Kit said in order to mask feelings she couldn't control. She entered the building that housed a great number of small individual booths. Occasionally she stopped to look at a trinket or two, well aware of Joshua's presence behind her. Finally she chose a pink-coral beaded necklace and haggled with the man until they were both satisfied with the price.

"Will you?" She handed her new purchase to Joshua. His fingers warmed her skin, his touch soft as he fastened the necklace around her neck. As the coral beads settled into a position around her throat, rough fingertips began to knead her neck. "That feels wonderful."

"Just relax," Joshua murmured. "Let's make this vacation about relaxing. For both of us."

"Mmm-hmm." Experiencing the magic of his fingers, she would have agreed with almost anything he said. He was definitely a special man, and Kit knew that things were now, after this wonderful afternoon, somehow different, just as last night's kiss and its interruption had left him searching the ship for her.

Kit sighed as his fingers worked their magic on her neck. She had achieved that morning's goal and gotten close to Joshua. He was beginning to open up to her and tell her things that she knew would make a great story.

So why did she feel so bad? When Joshua removed his fingers, Kit groaned in disappointment. From the corner of her eye she watched him idly kick a pebble out of the way. If she could grow to adore Georgia she could grow to love Joshua Parker.

She balked. Absolutely not. She was not going to fall in love with Joshua Parker.

Love was not a crush, love was—well, heck, she didn't know. But it wasn't this, and whatever these feelings were, they complicated her whole position, her reason for being on the cruise in the first place.

She had a goal: she wanted her father to recognize her as an independent woman. She could not let Joshua distract her from that. No guilt! she told herself. Normally that mantra worked. Today it sounded hollow and false.

They walked to Christ Church Cathedral, each gazing in silent wonderment at the magnificent stained-glass window of Jesus Christ on the cross that arched behind the altar. Each of them signed the guest book, Kit's name underneath Joshua's, both addresses reading simply New York City, U.S.A.

Kit shivered, glad Joshua didn't notice. How could she tell him that seeing his signature right above hers, committed to the guest book for all eternity, made them seem more than an item, almost as if they were already a couple?

She could not let that happen. As they began to walk back down George Street toward Bay Street, Kit bit her lip. She didn't like the way the air had suddenly, unexplainably, gotten heavy around her heart.

Chapter Seven

The message light was flashing furiously when Kit returned to her cabin hours later. After Joshua had extracted a promise from her to attend the party that night, he had left to meet with Bill Davies. Kit had whiled away the afternoon by taking a nap at the pool.

She grimaced at the annoying red light. Despite her reservations, she picked up the phone and dialed the ship's voice mail system. As she feared, the messages were all from her father. Each one ordered her to call, and with each subsequent message she could tell he was getting angrier and angrier.

Her roommates hadn't returned, and instead of confronting her father, Kit called Eleni. She needed information, and Eleni was the best person to get it from.

"Kit! Finally!" Kit could hear the stress in Eleni's voice despite the crackling connection that was costing $6.95 a minute. "We've been trying to reach you all day."

"Sorry." Kit retrieved the overnight envelope she had tossed in her suitcase earlier that morning. She slid her forefinger under the flap. "I've been out spending time with Joshua Parker."

"Good, I think. You're father's been in my office all day. He's not happy with your newest *Tattler* photos. Flirting with a casino dealer *and* plastered in a kiss with Joshua Parker. Believe me, it was all I could do to convince him that he shouldn't fly down there and bring you home. I told him the stress would be bad for his heart."

"His heart is fine," Kit replied. "I'm going to get this story, Eleni. I need this story." More than I need Joshua Parker's kisses she didn't add. Her father would be in her life permanently. Someone of Joshua's type only wanted one thing and then he'd be gone.

"Kit, your father told me he's killing the story."

"Oh, please," Kit scoffed. "He's bluffing. He'll run it. He's a businessman. I'm going to write it and he's going to run it."

She heard the pause before her editor spoke. "Well, in that case, Kit, your butt is on the line. You'd better come through with something spectacular, or you can kiss your precious hide goodbye."

"You're kidding." Kit stopped opening the envelope. "Please be serious. He wouldn't fire me. I'm his daughter. He always forgives me."

"Do I sound like I'm kidding?"

"You're overreacting, and I deserve this chance to work! I'm tired of being treated like Daddy's little princess. I want to be independent! I'm sick of writing fluff and hiding behind the name of Carol Jones."

"Well, if you say so. Did the envelope get there?"

The doubt in Eleni's voice irked Kit. "It's right here. I'm opening it now." Kit angled the receiver and pulled some papers out. "Anything specific I should know?"

Again, hesitation. Didn't anyone believe in her anymore? "In that envelope is some little-known family background on Joshua Parker. I want you to explore that angle. Get into his past. That's where the scoop lies. Get to the bottom of the rumor that Joshua's leaving television writing all together to make amends to his father. He's taking up farming or something like that if you can believe it. Anyway, I want you to find out why. Fame and fortune to raise cows? I don't get it, so you need to. Got it?"

Kit got it, and when Eleni put it that way, Kit didn't like it. Despite her flamboyant antics, she didn't use or hurt people. By not having come clean with Joshua earlier about the interview, it would now be nearly impossible to get her credibility back if she did decide to tell him. Just what had she gotten herself into?

"I'll see what I find out, Eleni, but until then I'm keeping my options open."

"Kit." Eleni's tone was resigned. "Exposure is what this business is all about."

"Yes, but—"

"There are no buts, Kit. You decided to accept this assignment. Do it right or don't do it at all. I'll tell you what, decide after you read the material. Of course, it would please your father if you decided not to—oh, hell."

"Eleni? What is it?"

"Kit?" Kit's stomach churned as she recognized

her father's booming voice. "Katherine Eleanor O'Brien, I know that's you!"

She heard him cough as he came to the phone.

"Yes, Father. I'm here." Kit bit her lip and held the phone away from her ear, readying herself for the tirade she knew was coming.

"About time you called. I don't even want to speculate about what you were doing today, but I'd better not read about it in the morning. The past two days have been bad enough. Do you understand? I'm already the laughingstock at my club, and can you imagine how I felt talking to Blaine and his father? He's my best friend! I was humiliated."

"Yes, Father."

"Good." Over the line she heard his humph of acknowledgment. "Another thing, you and I are going to discuss Blaine when you return from this farce of a trip, do you understand? He still wants to marry you."

"Yes, Father." Kit knew that any future discussion would only be a one-sided lecture. Besides, she wasn't about to argue long-distance with her father about her decision not to marry Blaine. When her father had his mind set on something it was like moving a mountain.

"No more antics, Katherine. You've shamed this family enough. Your mother would be so disappointed in your actions if she was alive. Now, you stay away from that man and don't disappoint me again, understand? I've already killed the story."

"Yes, Father." Kit gritted her teeth as her anger bubbled up. Under pressure to prove herself to her father, her feelings for Joshua faltered and winged their way somewhere into the recesses of her subconscious. No way was she going to let her father kill the story. It was her last chance. He'd already blocked her every attempt to leave the family company and work for a competitor.

No, she had to cling to the one truth about her father. He was a businessman at heart, and if she delivered an exposé on the reclusive Joshua Parker, she was sure her father would make the sound business decision and run it.

So deliver it she would, and he would finally give her the respect she deserved.

"Kit?" Eleni's voice came through the static, and Kit felt relieved that her father had cut his lecture short. "Check in with me tomorrow, okay?"

"Okay." The line went dead, and Kit set the phone down. She slumped into the chair and put her head into her hands. Only then did the tear trickle down from the corner of her eye. Angrily she brushed it away.

Again she had chosen to say "yes, Father" when she knew her actions would be the exact opposite. Instead of standing her ground, she acted like a meek child whose word meant nothing, whose actions in public raised her father's ire. Another nasty catch-22, Kit thought bitterly. The press exaggerated most of her antics. As for the dog food antic, if Blaine had just accepted that her no meant no, then she wouldn't have had to resort to commando tactics to get his attention and convince him that she was serious about not marrying him.

Not that it had helped. Now after talking with her father, she knew that neither man yet believed her when she said she wasn't marrying Blaine. She'd have to prove she could be a serious journalist by impressing her father with a feature on Joshua Parker.

Kit thumbed through the stack of press releases and newspaper clippings Eleni had sent. Her editor's handwritten note told her to check out the first few newspaper articles. A few were even translated from French into English.

Kit scanned them quickly. "Oh, my God." She couldn't believe she had just spoken aloud, and self-consciously she looked around to confirm that the small cabin was still empty.

Eleni had circled the gossip column item, dated over ten years ago, in red pen. Next to it were her cryptic words. "Get the family angle."

Kit blinked and began to read:

Joshua DeBettencourt, son of the Honorable Gasper DeBettencourt and Angelina Parker, the American heiress, has defied his father and left the university after being videotaped at a local strip club doing improvisations and singing karaoke with a naked showgirl. It is unconfirmed how much the younger DeBettencourt drank, but he needed a taxi home, a taxi he shared with two showgirls. The elder statesman, who is up for a Canadian Senate post, is one of the Québecois determined to keep Canada a unified country. Sources close to the elder DeBettencourt describe him as humiliated and utterly disappointed in his only son, and he refuses to acknowledge the boy's antics publicly. Word has it that they are not speaking, and that Joshua's mother called the elder statesman a bumbling idiot with no concept of how to treat their son.

Kit pushed aside the clipping and picked up the next one, from an American paper. The *Tattler* gossip column was approximately nine years old and written by a Mary Lynn Ross. Kit sighed. Mary Lynn had often gotten mileage out of Kit. Mary Lynn notoriously tainted stories, and Kit doubted that this one would contain much truth.

Joshua Parker, heartthrob writer of the surprise hit *Last Frontier,* is actually spurned Canadian aristocracy. His father, Gasper DeBettencourt, the prime minister's right-hand man, no longer speaks to his son. Their split, which is over two years old, occurred after Joshua refused to follow the path his father had preordained. In defiance, Joshua legally changed his surname to his mother's maiden name, Parker. Most Americans are familiar with Angelina Parker Cooper, the industrial heiress and travel guide author. She shamed the elder statesmen enough when she divorced DeBettencourt and left her son and two daughters behind to live with their father for six months each year. Single, Joshua has been seen on the arms of many beautiful women, but none of them have been able to land him for long. Not about to produce an heir for his father anytime soon, Joshua told me that he didn't care if he was disinherited and when his father wanted to talk to him he knew where to find him. A college dropout, to the disgust of his father, Joshua is writing and directing the new television series, *Last Frontier*....

The article went on, but Kit just put it down. Joshua Parker had a worse relationship with his father than she did with hers. And she had to expose Joshua's destructive relationship if she wanted to show her own father she was independent and worthy of serious stories.

Suddenly she wanted to throw up. There had to be a way to write this story and have her cake and eat it, too. She had to be able to earn her father's approval and have Joshua Parker for the duration of the cruise. She lifted her head in determination. She'd never failed before.

The fact that neither her father nor Joshua had any idea about her story plans made it easier for Kit to rationalize her decision. Everything would work out in the end. It always did. Right?

Kit studied the articles, finding more about the man she had spent the day with. According to them Joshua had never completed college and had worked at a variety of odd corporate jobs that his mother had found for him. His big break had come with creating *Last Frontier,* and after the first fan event, Joshua the heartthrob had emerged. The fans loved the writer of the show as much as the actors in it.

Then abruptly the press articles had stopped as

Joshua had become reclusive. Except for the occasional press release, there was only a blurb saying Joshua's father had undergone a kidney replacement. Other than that, personal information about Joshua had dried up.

Stomach queasy despite the delicious room service dinner she'd eaten, at ten minutes to nine Kit put on her makeup and surveyed her appearance in the mirror.

Kit had decided to let the dress speak for itself, not bothering to adorn it with any accessories except for the dangling silver earrings she wore. With short black almost cap sleeves, the dress covered more skin than her dress of the previous evening. Yet the dress, with a simple rounded neckline and a slightly flared A-line skirt stopping just below her knees, screamed notice me. Black sheer fabric was layered over a solid black lining creating a tone-on-tone effect. She blotted her lips with a toilet paper square and puckered to give herself a kiss of confidence that she didn't feel. She could do this. She would pull this off, without telling Joshua about the story she planned to write until it was done.

Time for the *Last Frontier*.

WHEN KIT ARRIVED people already crammed the room. Fans stood around in various costumes that Kit couldn't begin to describe if she had to. Georgia, Becca and Paula belonged to a fan group calling themselves drifters. At least that costume was simple, just khaki pants and blue denim shirts. Kit stood in the doorway, scanning the large one-level lounge.

Joshua stood at the opposite end of the room, wearing black, and she saw her roommates down front.

Kit unclenched her fists to relieve her stress. She could do this. With the poise she didn't feel, she walked steadily down toward them.

I'm not using him, Kit told herself. I'm going to put everything right. Just wait and see.

"There you are, sugar!" Dressed in her drifter khakis, Georgia came up and hugged Kit. "You look great. Doesn't she look great, everyone? It's time to knock Joshua off his feet, dear." Georgia reached for her wineglass. "And none of us will be offended if you don't come home tonight. We'll all just be dreaming we were you."

"Georgia!" Kit's face flushed a bright crimson as she sank into a chair. Her knees wobbled at the thought of making love to Joshua Parker. She might desire it, but it would be a mistake.

By now the party was in full gear. Designed to run informally, it appeared to be one big wedding reception with everyone in costume. The music pounded, people danced, and conversation hummed through the room.

"Great dress." A familiar, husky voice reached her ears, and instantly every hair on her body sizzled to attention.

Kit turned to face Joshua, and her heart plummeted to her feet. He appeared pleased, yet his eyes held something more, almost a wanton desire mixed with relief that she had appeared.

He surveyed her from head to toe. She knew he missed nothing, especially not the fact that the outer layer of the dress was see-through, the black layer underneath making the flowers prominent. Joshua drew in a long, slow breath before speaking.

"You look beautiful."

Kit swallowed as her mouth suddenly went dry. There was definitely something magical in how the low lights danced off his brown hair, revealing subtle reds that had previously gone unnoticed. His hair was pushed back away from his heart-shaped face, falling down in waves behind his ears to reveal his powerful cheekbones, his sharp jaw and his full lips. His hair cascaded down to his shoulders, yet it did not fall forward but rested on the black leather jacket that covered the black knit shirt.

Black. Beneath that black shirt lay his cool, creamy skin.... Kit bit her lip as her eyes surveyed the clean cut of the jacket, the easy fit of his pants, and the hard lines of his muscular, lithe body complementing well-designed clothes. The truth hit her. She wanted this man.

She locked her gaze with his and realized he'd sensed her appraisal. Kit felt she was drowning in his murky eyes, and she shifted in her chair, planting her feet firmly on the ground. But her body ignored her protest and her lips parted slightly. As heat flooded her veins, she knew it was hopeless. Her body had made its decision, even if her heart was afraid. She wanted to be in his arms.

"Dance?" Joshua asked as a slower song began playing.

Kit fought for a neutral voice. "I guess."

Joshua swept her to her feet and away to the dance

floor with confidence of a man no one ever turned down.

"Don't they make a cute couple?" Paula asked the group remaining at the table.

"That they do." Georgia let her gaze trail over to Joshua and Kit. The buzz had already started in the room. Georgia observed the whispers and stares of the crowd as Joshua and Kit began dancing to a second song. A pleased smile crossed Georgia's face. They made a good couple, even if they didn't even know it themselves yet.

Georgia watched as Joshua led Kit by the hand back to the table. Everyone might think she, Georgia, was a ditz, but it was all an act to hide her keen observations. She knew what she saw, too, Georgia told herself. And right now what she saw was Joshua's hand helping Kit into her seat, pushing her chair in and then running his fingers lightly across the back of her shoulders as he took a seat next to her.

"So how was dinner?" Joshua asked.

"Fine," Georgia replied, noting the way Joshua's hand played idly with Kit's fingertips. "Kit, I ordered you some soda. After last night I thought you'd want to avoid alcohol."

Gee, did everyone know she'd been hung over? Figured. They probably thought her a lush, when in fact she rarely drank. Kit gave Georgia a wry smile and reached for the glass of soda Georgia handed her. "Thanks."

"No problem." Georgia glanced at her watch and turned her attention to Paula. She gave Joshua and Kit exactly five minutes before they couldn't take being in public anymore. Too bad she hadn't placed a bet, but no one would have wagered, given the odds.

"WE'VE BEEN FORGOTTEN." Joshua leaned over and whispered in Kit's right ear as Georgia engaged Paula in conversation.

"Is that good or bad?" Kit turned her head to face Joshua, catching her breath as she did. His mouth was a scarce three inches from hers. His lips parted slightly, the simple, small movement releasing an earthquake through her body. Her mouth poised in a silent *o* as she waited for his answer.

"It's an opportunity to escape." Joshua rose gracefully to his feet, and Kit followed his movement as if her body was attached to his by an invisible magnetic force. Her right hand trembled in his left one as Joshua led her back to the dance floor.

The disc jockey lowered the lights for the slow number, and Joshua pressed the entire length of Kit's body against his. She wrapped her arms up around his neck, and his arms slid around her lower back.

Although centered on the dance floor in the midst of the crowd, Kit felt as if they were totally alone. Her head rested tenderly on his chest, and she could feel the rhythmic thumping of his heart. Their feet moved in a slow, sensual rhythm to the music, a seductive background noise now seeming distant. All she could hear was Joshua's heartbeat and hers, beating in unison.

A flashbulb popped.

She jumped as reality reared its ugly head. Joshua reacted to her sudden tension, but instead of allowing her to pull away, he tightened his grip. When his left hand snaked out to lift her chin, she found herself staring into his eyes.

"It's okay." His low husky voice soothed her ears, and he replaced his left hand on her back, his touch warming her skin. "If I can deal with it you can. I'll help."

Kit didn't understand his calm attitude. Filled with tumultuous emotion, she tried to pull herself away. "No, I can't deal with any more reporters. My father already yelled at me today about our front cover photo."

"It's only a dance." Joshua tightened his grip and pulled her closer. How she wanted the security he offered.

"You don't understand." She bit her lip. How could she tell him that she'd compromised her whole position, her whole reason for being on the cruise? She'd never be anything but Daddy's little girl. She wouldn't even be allowed to be Carol Jones. Not after more photos of her and Joshua surfaced.

"It's okay," he soothed. "I saw the paper at the staff meeting. I know all about Marilyn Roth and her millions of pseudonyms, one of which is Mary Lynn of the *Tattler*."

"My father told me I can't get any more press," Kit admitted. She attempted to focus, Joshua's heavenly arms short-circuiting her brain. "He was quite adamant when I talked to him earlier today."

"Ah, your father. The one you try to impress with antics that always seem to backfire. Tonight you need to decide what is it that you want."

Kit stared at him. What was it that she wanted? Suddenly she didn't know. Which was more important, her story or Joshua? One was her future, one was what? Surely Joshua wasn't her future. No, he was a fantasy, something she wanted but she couldn't have, shouldn't have.

He must have sensed what she was thinking. "I want you, Kit. More than anything else." His husky voice delivered the words that shattered all of Kit's mental jockeying.

For at that moment there was only one truth, one answer. She wanted him with every fiber of her being. This was the man. The man she wanted to make love with for the first time. The revelation made her body tense, and she tried to slip out of his grasp. When Joshua simply tightened his arms, Kit attempted one last protest.

"You don't understand. I really need to tell you about—" she began. He cut her off and she never finished telling him about the story.

"Let me speak. I know all about your antics, Kit, and don't worry. I've always been fascinated with you. Every picture, every article, I read them all without understanding why. When I saw you on the plane, my first thought was, wow." Joshua fingered the sheer black dress, and rubbed one of the flowers against the silky smooth layer underneath. "You drive me crazy, Kit, and I don't care who knows how much I want to make love to you. And we will make love, Kit. It's only a matter of finding the right time."

"I...I..." Kit found herself stammering at his confident disclosure. "I need to tell you something."

"It will keep until tomorrow, Kit, but I won't." His chuckle was low and husky. "This dress is sexier than the one you wore last night. If we don't get out of here now, they'll really have some photo ops."

Through the layers of her dress, his fingers toyed with the thin bra strap on her back. It was simply too much. All thoughts of telling him about the story she was writing vanished as a tremor bolted through her body. As Joshua moved his hands to safer ground at the curve of her back, she was grateful for the darkness.

His mouth hovered dangerously close to hers and ardent desire overpowered her as he leaned forward to capture her mouth lightly before lifting his lips away. Her lips tingled and opened, softened with a desire that had been long denied. Joshua's lips moved again. His breath tickled her ear as his words tumbled out. "I want you, Kit."

Speech failed her. Already she was on fire, her spirit drawn like a moth to a flame just from his kiss. She opened her mouth to reply, but he silenced her with another touch of his lips to hers. The brief kiss ignited Kit's whole body, and it exploded into fireworks. Joshua had some awareness of time, and he moved her into a respectable posture as the song ended and the bright strobe lights began to undulate with the beat of the fast dance.

Words were unnecessary as Joshua led Kit off the dance floor, which was good because Kit didn't know if she could sound coherent. Heat seared through her body as his fingers cupped her elbow. They walked toward the opposite side of the room from her table, and she accompanied him into the hall.

"We're cutting out early," he told her, "no matter how much Bill insists the cast has to stay until the end. You're worth every bit of his wrath."

"Look, I've got to tell my roommates."

"They'll understand."

The bright lights hit them, and Kit blinked. Was he Pan of Greek mythology? He led. She followed. Her cabin was two decks down, but once inside the lift Joshua instead pressed the button for up, and the doors opened on the bridge deck. Kit was bewildered, but he propelled her forward, through the short hallway along the leeward side as they headed toward the bow of the ship.

Kit remained silent as Joshua inserted his pass card and opened stateroom 9134. Not only was his room almost one-third bigger than hers, but it had one bed, not four, a king-size one delightfully turned down.

But Joshua led her past the bed, and within seconds they had stepped out through the sliding glass doors and onto the private balcony. The warm breeze blew across her face, lifting strands of her hair. A solid wall on each side privatized the balcony, and the sundeck above made the roof. He remained mute, his only movement a raising of his eyebrows as if he had a secret. He left Kit to her thoughts as he returned inside for a moment, and she studied the dark, distant point where the starry night came down to caress the sea beyond.

Joshua came back with two glasses and a tiny bottle of what looked like champagne. When she saw it was sparkling grape juice, Kit nodded her surprised approval and sat on one of the small white chairs.

He gave her a wicked grin. "Minibar. Dastardly things. But they do in a pinch." With a flourish he placed the four-inch-tall round water glasses on the table and proceeded to pop open the bottle.

"If I had the proper glasses you would have known I was planning this." Bubbles popped as he poured, and the bottle emptied before it filled the two glasses. "I know, not a lot, but I can order more if you want."

"No." Kit quickly shook her head and smiled. "This is perfect. Very thoughtful actually, considering I still think there's vodka floating in my system from last night. I'm still wondering why I drank that. I usually hate vodka."

Joshua stretched and his left leg brushed Kit's. "Perhaps you were afraid of what you wanted."

Kit started slightly, reaching for the glass Joshua held out. Could he see through her? No, it was just the contact with his leg causing her to jump.

He lifted his glass in a toast, and Kit followed suit. The lines around his brown eyes crinkled deliciously, and Kit attempted to relax.

"What will your pleasure be, Kit O'Brien?" Joshua rubbed his leg deliberately against hers, and her bones melted.

She fought his innate appeal and took a gulp of grape juice. Bubbles burst against the back of her throat. "You are a devil."

Joshua winked at her description. "Perhaps. Humor me. Why?"

"Let's see. Chasing me last night, luring me up here tonight, making us press fodder."

"The ugly press." Joshua leaned forward and set his glass on the table. His tone changed from playful to serious. "I've told you I don't care who knows how much I want you."

Kit swallowed. "That's good, since they probably got great shots of us on the dance floor."

He shrugged. "Despite my aversion to the press, I'll risk it. I want you that much."

Kit's hand stilled in midair and no words came forth.

Joshua wet his lower lip, and Kit stared at his tongue, fascinated.

"So," he said, pausing for what seemed like an indeterminable second. "There is only one question, Kit O'Brien."

A gentle gust of wind lifted Kit's hair. "What's that?"

"It's whether you want me enough. Because I want to make love to you more than I've wanted anything or anyone else, and I'm willing to throw caution to the wind to do it. I'm not going to let you leave just because you're afraid." He gazed at her, his eyes not flickering. Kit sharply sucked in her breath.

Even though they'd just met, here was a man who understood her, who knew her better than her closest friends.

Joshua stood and took the bottle and empty glasses back into the cabin. Alone, Kit rose, and placed her hands on the railing. She gripped the balcony rail and stared out at the midnight-blue sea. How did she feel? Was she willing to risk her father's continued wrath?

She stared out across the infinite blackness, trying to draw from it some of its infinite peace. While she generated a lot of press since she never went out with anyone past a third date, most of it was untrue. She had never found someone she wanted to make love to. But here on this balcony, she knew that fact had changed. The press could be hanged; the reporters would speculate she'd made love with Joshua, because she'd been seen with him more than once.

And he was positively scintillating. Positively perfect. The stars twinkled brighter, and Kit drew in a deep breath.

Tonight, tonight she needed Joshua Parker. Needed him to make love to her. Needed him to change her from a childish girl into a loving, fulfilled woman.

Tomorrow she would figure out what to do about her father and his wrath. Tomorrow she could deal with the story she now didn't have any desire at all to write, the story she wouldn't ever write now, no matter what the consequence to her career. Tomorrow she could figure out another way to earn her father's respect. But not now.

No, tonight was just going to be about her and Joshua. Like Scarlett O'Hara she would deal with sorting everything out some other day. But not tonight.

Behind her, Joshua returned to the balcony. She turned around and reached her hands out for him. Joshua took them and pulled Kit to him.

"I want you to be sure, Kit." Joshua's breath was raspy as if his own control was precarious.

"I'm sure." Kit's strong voice sounded foreign to her ears. Impatient for his lips to finally claim hers, when she saw the heat in his eyes, a fire began between her thighs and spread up to her belly. She was beyond ready. "I want you, Joshua Parker." She saw his brown eyes widen with overwhelming desire.

Then his lips crushed down, his tongue pushing past her lips in its need to possess her mouth. Kit laced her arms around his neck, and she pressed her full length against his hard body. Every inch of his need throbbed, and her own fire was not to be quenched. Joshua freed himself from her mouth and ran kisses around the entire front of her neck before pulling away from her with a groan.

"We've got to slow down," Joshua said, his voice deep with desire. "If I don't I won't be able to keep my hands from shredding this dress right off you."

An alien, devilish delight spread through her. She moved closer to him and tilted her face up to his. The movement of her legs brushed against his manhood, and with an uncontrolled groan Joshua pushed her back against the dividing wall between the balconies.

"Vixen." He breathed heavily, his mouth pressing on her neck lightly, teasingly. "You're driving me absolutely mad."

Kit curled her fingers into his hair. "I want you, Joshua," she whispered, voice filled with rapturous desire. "I want you to kiss me until I can't stand it anymore."

Her lips parted slowly, subtly beckoning, calling him to take another taste.

Joshua's eyes searched her face, and he suddenly swooped in to kiss her neck again. The heat immediately raced through Kit, and she pulled Joshua to her, her lips finding his neck. Joshua pushed his arms out straight and again backed away from her.

"This is wrong," he said.

Chapter Eight

Kit's eyes flew open. "What?" Her voice was thick with disbelieving desire.

"No, Kit." Joshua tried to explain. "Your clothes. Tomorrow morning."

"What?" Confused, Kit was getting upset.

Joshua groaned and tried again. "You need a change of clothes. For the morning." Joshua reached forward and lifted her chin. "If you creep through the ship in your evening clothes tomorrow morning, the press will really have a field day. Let's get your clothes now. Then you can stay with me. Wake up in my arms. Shower with me."

Understanding softened Kit's face as she realized what he was saying. "Mmm." She leaned forward to try to kiss him again. "So where am I going to get these clothes?"

Joshua leaned forward to answer the call of her sensual mouth. His lips caressed hers, depositing feathery kisses in between the tickling of his tongue. Kit arched forward and opened her lips to try to capture his mouth fully, but Joshua evaded her and backed away. "Your cabin. Clothes. Now."

"I guess you were serious when you said you hadn't planned this," she said.

He gave her another deep kiss, his breath ragged as he pulled away. "No, but I am planning this now." Grabbing her hand, he pulled her from the deck, through his room and out into the hall.

Kit giggled as Joshua's hand slid down her back and across her bottom. She pressed the elevator button for the A deck. "Hey, what if they catch us now?"

"It'll be better than if they catch you in your evening dress in the morning."

"True." Her eyes widened as Joshua turned her to face him. He pressed her back against the wall of the aftmost lift as his mouth slid down her neck. His arms lifted up her dress slightly and he caressed her left thigh. Kit arched her leg up onto his hip and Joshua slid his palm up, under her dress, to cup her bottom in his hand. Only the shudder of the elevator as it came to a stop caused them to separate.

"Thank heaven your cabin is close."

Kit fumbled with the key, and Joshua wordlessly took it from her and opened the door. Once inside she went straight to work, simply grabbing her toothbrush, a hairbrush, a pair of shorts, sandals, a T-shirt and clean undergarments. She threw them all into a small plastic *Island Voyager* bag.

"I'm ready." She noticed Joshua had eaten her mint off of her pillow. "Hey! That was my mint!"

"Here." Joshua grabbed her and yanked her to him. "I'll share."

Kit understood his meaning as his lips pressed urgently down upon hers. Her mouth opened instantly, allowing his to again possess and claim her. Her knees wobbled, and he leaned her back against the cabin door, his fingers clenching the flimsy back outer layer of her dress. Kit's left hand still clutched the bag, and she threaded her right hand into his wavy brown tresses.

With extreme possession of will, Joshua pulled away from her. "We need to get out of here."

"Mmm-hmm." Kit opened her eyes slowly, still savoring his kiss and the mint. She crunched the last of it. "Should I leave a note?"

"They'll figure it out if they haven't already." Joshua gripped the door and flung it open. "Trust me."

"Absolutely." Kit couldn't remember how they got back to his cabin. There had been only one other couple in the elevator, and the man and his wife had gotten off just one deck above Kit's. Although no other souls passed Kit and Joshua in the hall, her adrenaline pumped until they finally made it safely back to his cabin.

Kit dropped her bag the second she was through the door. The shoes inside clunked to the floor, but Kit paid them no heed. She turned her face eagerly toward his.

She was not denied. Joshua's lips immediately found hers. Freed from her mental restraint, Kit kissed him back. Her tongue explored his mouth, tasting each crevice. Joshua's fingers journeyed over Kit's skin, tracing the curve of her neck, the indentations behind her ears and the smoothness of her jawbone.

She could swim in his kisses forever, but she broke free, arching her head back and sending Joshua's lips flaming down the satiny skin of her throat. His lips played with her neck as his hands found her waist. His tongue teased at the neckline of her dress, darting below it. Kit arched her back forward. Her skin changed from hot to cold to hot, and Joshua slid his hands upward, cupping her breasts as they rose to meet him.

A small cry escaped her mouth, and his hands slid around to her zipper. Inch by inch the zipper slid smoothly down the track, and Joshua locked his gaze onto Kit's. He placed both hands on the neckline of her dress and began to ease the black garment from her shoulders. As the dress dropped to the floor Joshua broke eye contact with her. She closed her eyes, opening them only as she heard his shocked intake of breath.

"Ma belle! Kit!"

She found his gaze wondrous as he brought his lips back to her mouth. He kissed her mouth thoroughly before stepping back to look at her again.

She stood before him in nothing but black lace. Her spaghetti-strap bra was cut low, the lacy cups hardly covering her full breasts. Her nipples strained to escape the material that barely hid them. Joshua's gaze slid down her smooth stomach, finding the French-cut underwear that was high in the thigh, yet dipped dangerously and decadently low in the front and back. Kit's black hose had lace tops that connected to the black, lacy, midthigh garters of the black garter belt circling her waist. Joshua met Kit's smoldering, waiting green eyes. She could see it on his face before his words reached her ears. "*Ma chérie.* You are beautiful."

His passion heightened, and her body quickened with pleasure as his hands moved forward to caress her bare, silky shoulders. His lips moved back over her skin, tasting her creamy flesh on his journey down the valley between her breasts. Joshua's hands eased the straps down, his fingers searing her skin as they cupped her breasts. Through the thin layer of fabric his touch sent fire racing through her body. Her own need grew, throbbed, and her hands moved to remove his jacket.

He interrupted her, moving to scoop her up and carry her to the already turned-down bed. "Thank heaven for cabin stewards."

He smelled delightful, but now he was too far away. She responded by reaching up to pull his head down toward hers.

Joshua grazed past her lips, instead bending his head to run his tongue under the lacy bra. The act flared lightning flashes across her brain. She groaned with rapture when he finally pushed the bra down and brought her nipple firmly between his lips. His tongue lightly circled, pulling, tweaking, teasing, and she fisted the back of his shirt, her clenched fingers pulling on him as waves of pleasure bounded over her. His fingers and mouth worked their earth-shattering magic. Frenzied passion invaded her as he teased her breasts, blowing ever so gently to cool, and then covering her again with the heat of his mouth.

Finally Joshua lifted his head, and her eyes slowly

opened. Drugged with fire, she smiled at him, a sensual cat-like pleased smile.

"Help me, Kit."

He spoke softly, yet there was no questioning his urging. She leaned up, her fingers instantly finding the buttons of his black shirt. At last the barrier to his flesh disappeared. With a newfound boldness she undid her bra and tossed it aside. A wanton smile crossed his lips as his gaze roved over her body. Yet there was no embarrassment as she simply laced her arms around his neck, and as her mouth found his, she pulled him back down on top of her.

His naked flesh connected directly with hers, and heat waves rolled over her. She fumbled with his trousers, her hands reaching their intended target as she pushed the restraining clothing away.

He quivered as her fingers finally found him, her touch fragile, unsure and then growing bolder and confident as she recognized the severity of his need for her. His fingers played with the inside of her thighs, and a husky, low cry escaped from her lips as Joshua unhooked her garter belt clips.

His fingers slid over the lacy fabric of her black panties, and his hand pressed into the mound above her womanhood. He caressed her gently, rubbing with the fabric, teasing her to be sure. He slipped his fingers underneath the lace, touching her heat, stroking her lightly.

Her need for him overtook her like a freight train, and her eyes flew open as passionate desire overwhelmed her. She lowered her eyelashes slowly, calling him, and his fingers lifted away the last lacy barriers before he stopped.

Kit felt his coiled tension, understood his desperate restraint. Again she reached forward to lace her arms around his neck and pull his lips to hers. This time she possessed him: leading him, guiding him, her body arching and calling him to her. "Joshua!"

With a swift movement he ripped the foil packet and prepared himself. He drove himself deeply into her and her body detonated into slivery fragments of glistening pleasure.

Joshua's head came up, surprise evident. His lips opened, and his face mirrored the exquisite nature of their union. Her body rocked under his, and she matched his rhythm and urged him on, her legs wrapped tightly around him as she peaked. His name escaped from her lips, and her hands flew up into the brown hair that cascaded past his face. She knit her fingers into the brown silky locks, threading and weaving her fingers through it, her urgency of desire driving him even further into ultimate ecstasy.

United, they reached the last pinnacle together, the room erupting into millions of brilliant little stars as their bodies crescendoed. Her body shuddered and quaked, and she melted down into the sheets, drawing Joshua to rest on top of her. Her hands caressed his back as his lips nibbled on the side of her neck. The weight of him was still upon her, and slowly he lifted his head to look at her.

"Kit." He could only whisper her name, but it was enough. "I didn't know. I was too rough."

She gazed at him. He knew what she had done,

what gift she had chosen to share just with him. Her body was warm with emergent love, and she reached up a finger and traced his mouth. His lips tugged gently on her fingertip.

"I'm not all my reputation says," she said, trying to make light of giving him her virginity.

He'd have none of it. "Did I hurt you?"

"No." She writhed and twisted beneath him, and fire flared. Joshua's lips again caressed her fingertip. She groaned and reached up to pull his head back down, stopping his lips directly above her awaiting mouth. Her voice was heated, low and sensual. "Look what you've created, Joshua Parker."

Joshua's body, poised just inches from hers, hardened with rekindled desire. He crushed his lips down upon hers. "Ditto, Kit O'Brien."

KIT AWOKE WITH A START. The hum of the ship's engines had stopped, indicating that the *Island Voyager* had reached its final port of call, the private island.

Despite the fact that dawn had not yet fully begun to seep in from the still-open drapes, Kit shifted slightly, her body still protectively curled up beneath Joshua's firm arms. He cradled her gently, and he tightened his grip as she moved to look at him.

In the stillness of the remnants of the night Kit could see him, his face highlighted from the glow of the thin pink sliver of morning sky. His face had relaxed in sleep, and she reached out a finger to trace it. Lightly she touched him, running her finger across his brows and down to touch lips still swollen from the passion of their lovemaking. Unconsciously his mouth opened to kiss her finger, and Kit pulled it gently away.

Her body remained naked beside his, and she ran her finger over the ridge of his shoulder. A soft, satisfied smile crossed her face as he pulled her closer, crushing her toward him before he drifted further into deep sleep.

She'd heard horror stories of first-time experiences from college friends, and Kit had shied away, never knowing that lovemaking could be so fulfilling, so wonderful. Joshua had explored parts of her body that she hadn't known would react with the pleasure they did. He had found crevices and turned them into valleys of desire. Kit sleepily closed her eyes again and sighed in wonder. So this was what love was all about.

Love? Her eyes flew open in shock. She was suddenly wide awake. What had she just thought? Love? Surely not!

Kit stared at Joshua Parker with renewed interest. People didn't fall in love this fast except on television. It was like that wedding magic, when people met and fell in love during someone's wedding reception. They fell out of love equally as fast. Even if Joshua cared a little, if she told him the true reason she'd been sent on the cruise, he would drop her like a hot potato. No, it was better he just thought she was escaping her father.

The force of what she'd done hit her. She had just made love with the man Eleni expected her to interview! She'd compromised her whole credibility.

Sure, she'd decided last night that there would be

no story, and at some point she'd have to tell Eleni that. Still, her editor wouldn't see it as Kit obeying her father. No, Eleni would see it as Kit compromising herself with her subject. So much for respect. But she had wanted him.

Maybe she had since the beginning of time. She didn't know. She turned to watch him, and her body quickened. Her senses already longed for him, called for him. Her fingers wanted to roam and caress his body. Her lips wanted to travel all over curves she hadn't discovered the night before. Her tongue wanted to again taste the musky essence that was entirely his. Her legs wanted to wrap around him and possess him. A shudder of desire trembled through Kit. She wanted to make love to him again.

With Joshua she felt complete. Whole. One. Not just satisfied sexually, although she had definitely been that. There had been more to their lovemaking, and her heart knew it, despite her head's denial. While she certainly knew she wasn't in love with him, the truth of it was, whatever these emerging feelings were petrified her.

But one thing she was sure of, she was not going to fall in love with Joshua Parker. Lust maybe, but not love.

Sunlight began to seep into the cabin, slowly at first, and then quickly, as if it were water enlarging an opening. The natural highlights in Joshua's hair shimmered, and Kit's heart jumped to her throat.

What had she just done? How was she going to fix it? She had to get out of his cabin. She had to get away from him. Now. Quickly she swallowed back desperate tears and began the slow, arduous task of extracting herself without waking him up.

She had never crept out of a man's bed before, but she had been cursed with roommates in college who slept lightly. She planted her feet on the floor and pulled the clothes out of the bag she'd retrieved from her cabin last night. With deft fingers she scooped up the black dress, her shoes and lingerie and tossed it into the bag. Jewelry. Where was it? Kit couldn't remember, and a furtive glance didn't locate it. Joshua stirred suddenly, and in a split decision Kit left the items behind as she slid quietly out of his cabin and headed for her own.

JOSHUA HAD KNOWN Kit was up as soon as the warmth of her body had left his. He had held her protectively all night, nestling her in the curve of his arms. Several times while he slept his eyes had flown open, and he had checked to see if she was there. Now the watch glowing ominously next to the bed told him that it was only 6:25 in the morning. He had only been able to hold Kit for mere hours past their lovemaking. With a grim heart Joshua realized it wasn't enough.

Their lovemaking could only be described as beautiful, and even *beautiful* did not depict it. With Kit Joshua had seen the female body as if he were viewing it for the first time. There was something about her, something she drew from his being that no other woman had ever come even close to locating. He had wanted Kit more than any other woman he had ever met. Touching her was more than passion. It made him complete, somehow whole.

He remembered how she looked as he had explored her body, her eyes closed and her face lit with rapture. His fingers had played ever so gently, pressing, exploring, tantalizing, and still he had continued to watch her, deriving his greatest pleasure from viewing her body respond to the new sensations and seeing the subsequent emotions cross her face.

He had never done that before—watch a woman—and now he understood why. The act itself was so intimate, so personal. This time he knew he was giving not only absolute delight, but that he was witness to it, privy to her intimate secrets. He had never wanted to cross that barrier with any woman, except with Kit. Now that he had crossed it, he didn't want to lose her. Not yet. There was so much he could teach her about lovemaking, so much more he wanted to give to her, to share with her.

She had been a virgin, New York City's tabloid queen, and she had chosen him to be her first lover. He smiled. He had branded her his, last night, and for the first time in his life he had felt complete. The sudden insight hit him. Who would have guessed his thoughts from yesterday would be so wrong?

Maybe Kit was the one who could understand him, who could respect the relationship he had with his father because of her own.

They fitted so well together, and he knew he could show her how to put things right. He'd made the mistakes she was growing through, and he could save her so much pain.

And he wanted to. He didn't know where they would end up, but he knew this wasn't just some cruise magic.

They might be oil and vinegar, city girl to country boy, but right now the fire was too hot to extinguish, and he didn't want to.

But she had slipped away, like a thief from his bed.

Kit! Joshua groaned and rolled over to bury his head in his pillow. He could still smell her presence on the sheets, and it drove him mad. *Kit, I wanted to hold you. To wake up with you. To make love to you again. To feed you breakfast in bed.*

Not to have you slip away from me like a dream. Joshua tossed once more, this time to stare at the chalk-white ceiling. He wasn't going to let her go. It would not end like this.

Not when Kit occupied his thoughts. How had she wrapped him around her finger, a feat no other woman had ever accomplished? She didn't know it, instead, slinking away as if she were ashamed of her passion. As if she were a one-night stand, something he'd already determined she would not be. Joshua made fists and pounded on the bed before he sat upright with a newfound determination. He leaped naked from the bed and headed for the shower with only one thought—to bring Kit O'Brien back to his bed, by whatever means necessary.

Chapter Nine

The *Tattler,* Saturday, Nov. 23
Mary Lynn's About the Town
Kit'ten Finds New Fish to Play with

Just remember readers, you heard it here first!
Kit O'Brien lives up to the adage that there are
other fish in the sea. Just two days after dumping dog food on her fiancé, Blaine Rourke, she
not only kissed Joshua Parker (see photo page
one), but spent the night in his cabin! Every
LaFrofan attending the costume party on the *Island Voyager* cruise ship saw the kiss and the
couple's passionate disappearance. They never
returned to the party. Hmm. A new lover, one
more notch on Kit's bedpost. I wonder what her
father thinks of this?

He couldn't believe it. No, he could, he just didn't
believe she had the nerve. With disgust, Michael
O'Brien tossed down the *Tattler.* The last thing he
needed or wanted with his Saturday-morning coffee
was to see his daughter plastered all over the front

page kissing Joshua Parker, with the accompanying trash Mary Lynn wrote making matters even worse.

"What did I do to deserve this?" he muttered aloud, attracting the attention of his son.

"What did you say, Father?" Cameron looked up from his bagel. His son had decided to join him for a late breakfast, his latest girlfriend now ancient history.

"This paper you brought me. I wondered what I did to deserve something like this. Carlton's going to have a fit." Michael shook his head as he thought of his best friend, Blaine's father. "Kit told me she understood. And now she defies me!"

"Oh, it'll be fine," Cameron soothed. He didn't appear at all concerned.

Michael frowned at his son. "You seem awfully chipper today. Gloating that it's not you in the papers?"

Cameron seemed to sober, but only for a moment before he grinned again. "Absolutely. Kit has never been this publicly outrageous before. At least there wasn't a photographer outside Saks when she threw paint on Mrs. Winterby's fur."

"Don't even remind me of that. What cause was that, Save the Minks or something? All I know is it cost me a small fortune to restore Mrs. Winterby's goodwill."

"Well, you lived through it. Hey, look on the bright side. Maybe she's in love with this guy. He seems like an okay sort. Maybe you can marry her off to him." Cameron gave his father a grin. Whenever Michael O'Brien concentrated on getting his daughter wed, the heat was off his son.

"Absolutely not!" His father shook with controlled rage. "She's just rebelling. She'll see the light as soon as I get her home."

"Of course." Cameron smiled, sensing some time-out from being under his father's matchmaking thumb. "Shall I get you the phone?"

"THIS IS JUST TOO EXCITING," Paula said. Behind her sunglasses, Kit blinked to attention. Her thoughts were in overdrive as she waited in the line for the ferry that would take passengers to the small island.

"I mean, can you believe it, Kit? I won the lunch with the cast. I've never won anything. I can't believe I was so lucky."

Kit kept quiet as the line moved forward. The only luck favoring her was that her roommates had still been asleep when she had returned to the cabin, and not one of them had asked her about her evening when they finally did wake up. She had showered since leaving Joshua, and Kit smoothed down the sleeveless button-up white shirt. Her fingers toyed with the exposed shirttails, and she scrunched one before letting it again drop over her blue denim shorts. If her roommates had left her a choice she would have stayed on the ship. Maybe get a facial at the spa. Anything to put off the inevitable of running into him.

"Did you wear a swimsuit?" Georgia suddenly asked.

"Um, no." Kit shifted her leather fanny pack. "I

heard that the water's a bit colder than normal for November.''

''Oh.'' Georgia fell into silence. Since the day was sunny, they chose seats on top of the two-level boat. Kit could see the island in the distance, and after passengers filled the boat to capacity, the boat began its short journey across the blue-green waters.

''What time is it?'' Paula asked.

''Almost noon,'' Becca replied. ''What time is your lunch?''

''Twelve-fifteen at the café.'' Paula smoothed out the little map of the island that the cruise line had given all the passengers. ''Let's see, once we arrive on the dock, we need to follow this wooden path. At the fork go left to the beach and right to the small village area.''

''Oh, that's easy to find.'' Georgia nodded. Kit tuned them out. She wondered if Joshua was already on the island, but brushed that thought aside when she disembarked. Instead she concentrated on assessing her surroundings.

The village consisted of a bunch of buildings constructed to look like old-fashioned tropical-paradise huts. Most of the huts were small gift stores. Some were large enough to walk inside, while others, such as the hut that sold film, beach toys and sunscreen, were simply ten-foot-square buildings open on one side to curious shoppers. Several large, open-air pavilions with wood plank floors contained bars, dance floors and dining tables. People who wanted could sign up for parasailing, snorkeling, banana-boat rides, arts and crafts or simply explore the island on their own, which was what Kit planned to do.

"Your lunch is over there." Georgia pointed to one of the large pavilions.

"Got it," Paula said. "I can't wait."

"This is so clever! I just love the way they created this," Becca exclaimed. She looked at the group. "Who's hungry, and who wants to check out the beach?"

"I can wait to eat," Georgia said. "Paula? Kit?"

"I've got a few minutes, let's see the beach first," Paula said. Kit shrugged and turned to follow them.

The beach was beautiful. The cruise line had placed blue and white umbrellas in a row, creating an illusion of umbrellas almost as far as the eye could see, even though the umbrellas ended after about one thousand feet. People already frolicked in the water, and several games of sand volleyball were in progress. The beach consisted of a good 150 feet of fine, pinkish coral sand, separating the water from the tropical foliage of the inner part of the island.

Paula's few minutes were up, and she and Georgia headed back toward the village.

Becca turned to Kit. "So, do you want to take part in any of the games?"

Kit surveyed the beach again, her eyes hidden by her designer sunglasses. A cruise attendant was handing out towels in the small hut a few feet in front of her.

"I don't think so. Why don't you go ahead and catch up with Georgia? I brought a book, and I'm going to commandeer one of those umbrellas." And maybe the sun will warm up this coldness that's settled over my heart, Kit didn't add.

"Are you sure?" Becca asked.

"Yeah," Kit nodded. "I need a bit of downtime. Go. I'll see you later."

"Okay." Becca shrugged and scurried off after Georgia.

Kit walked up to the small hut and reached for a free towel. "I can take any umbrella?"

"Ya." The attendant gave her a grin.

"What about the cabanas?" Kit pointed to the green-and-white-striped tents farther down the beach.

"Ya." The attendant nodded and smiled again. "Raft rental five dollar."

"No raft, thanks." Kit reached down to flip her sandals off and began to move along the row of umbrellas until she found an unoccupied one as far away from everyone else as possible. Kit spread the towel out and reached into her fanny pack for the romance novel she had brought with her.

"Why is my life so complicated?" Kit questioned the sand crab skittering by. "Why couldn't I just tell him, Joshua, I'm not like Marilyn Roth. I care about you, but in order for my father to believe I'm a serious journalist I needed to do a story on you. But I've changed my mind. Now I just want you. As if he'll believe that." Kit didn't even want to imagine what Joshua's reaction would be. "No. I can't tell him. Ever."

With a sigh she rolled over onto her stomach and dug her toes in the sand. She began to read, ignoring the flow of people who came and went as the day slipped into midafternoon.

At some point she fell asleep, and when she awoke she pressed a forefinger to her forearm. The sunblock had worked, and she hadn't burned. She picked up her towel and decided to walk down the beach a bit more. It was either that or return to the ship, and she wasn't in the mood to return to her room at three o'clock.

Fewer people now crowded the beach, and as Kit walked past the last cabana, she discovered it was empty. Deciding to get out of the direct sun, Kit walked inside the eight-by-six-foot structure and plopped her towel down. Sighing, she picked up her book again and buried her nose in someone else's love life for a while.

JOSHUA WATCHED the figure pick up her towel and walk down the beach. Even from a distance, he knew it was Kit. He had been hoping she'd come to find him, but had realized how unrealistic that wish was when she hadn't appeared to meet her roommates for lunch. So instead he had suffered through the *Last Frontier* events and, after pumping Georgia—who couldn't keep a secret to save her life—for information, Joshua had known every single one of Kit's movements since her return to her cabin that morning. Georgia had told him that Kit hadn't seemed herself. *I wonder why*, Joshua had thought with a knowing grin, which then had turned into a determined grimace.

He reached down and took off his leather Topsiders

and dug his toes into the sand. He'd thought about Kit on and off during the day. She needed nothing from him—nothing except him, Joshua the person. He'd been waiting his life to find someone like that. She was under his skin, and he wasn't ready to scratch the itch away yet. No, he owed it to himself to find her.

"So, ARE YOU GOING to avoid me the rest of the cruise?"

Joshua's extremely familiar voice tickled her ear. With a start, Kit jerked her head up, finding him squatting next to her. Her movement knocked him off balance, tipping him into the sand.

"Are you okay?" she asked.

"Yeah." Joshua gave her a cheeky grin, and Kit's heart melted. He stood up and brushed off the sand. "My turn to lose my balance. I've been following you since I saw you get up from the umbrella."

He sat at the foot of her towel. His thigh brushed hers, the tiny curled hairs on his leg electrifying her as he leaned closer. "I missed you this morning."

"I…" Kit's excuses fled. He reached forward and cupped her chin in his hand and brought her face up to his.

"Don't worry," his mouth whispered next to hers. "I think I understand why you left. Still, my shower was lonely. I had these visions of us, but I'd much rather show you than tell you."

He turned his face again, his lips grazing over her cheek before finding her awaiting mouth. His mouth plundered hers instantly, as if he craved a drink of water in the desert, and Kit's body instantly responded to the primitive call. She threw caution to the wind. After he found out about her secret he would never speak to her again. No, she wanted him too much to tell him. He never could know.

Her tongue probed into his mouth, returning his ardor as the kiss deepened. Joshua had explored all the crevices of her mouth the night before, yet Kit's brain exploded when he located new passion points. Finally his possession of her mouth ceased and he kissed the outside of her lips several times before backing away to look into her face.

"This is way too public a place to take this any further." Joshua groaned with frustration, but still he rubbed a forefinger down the inside of her right arm. The motion sent waves of desire through her.

When he moved that forefinger to her lips, Kit kissed it. She sucked gently and used her teeth to nip the end.

"Stop that!" Joshua's eyes darkened, and he pulled his finger away. "If you don't we're going to be on the next ferry back to the ship."

"What's stopping us?" Was that her voice, that husky, seductive sound? Her body was on fire, flaming from the sensations coursing through it. "I've got nowhere else I'd rather be. You could shut the ties, or we can take one of those overgrown paths that I saw earlier."

"Brazen little hussy," Joshua teased, leaning over to kiss her lightly on the nose. "Look what I've done. I've corrupted you. Who would have guessed you were such an innocent just last night?"

Kit reached up with both hands and pulled his head to hers. She only had now. Only now to take something she wanted for herself, like Joshua had urged her last night. "I like being corrupted. Especially by you." Her voice trailed off as she snaked an arm around his neck.

"Kit!" After a series of kisses Joshua pulled himself away from her mouth and leaned up on his arms to look at her face. He wanted her. Kit reveled in the thought. There was no mistaking his need, quite evident by the bulge in his shorts. His sandy legs intertwined with hers.

"We'll have to keep very quiet. None of that noise like last night," he teased.

"Scout's honor." Kit ran her hands underneath his shirt and across his flat nipples. Joshua groaned and pulled himself away from her.

"Were you even a scout?" Joshua went to the front of the cabana and tied the laces.

"No." But she knew it didn't matter, not to him, and especially not to her. Not now. Right now she needed him, needed his touch.

The view of the sea vanished as the cool darkness enveloped them. They were alone, with no way anyone could see. "Joshua," Kit cried softly, pulling him back down to her.

"Yes, darling," he whispered, his mouth placing kisses over her neck. "Is this what you want?"

"Oh, yes!" Kit shuddered with pleasure as Joshua's hands slid up under her shirt and up under the lace of her bra to caress her nipples. The hard buds pebbled even more, and Kit arched up, Joshua catching her lips with a kiss.

He lifted her shirt up and his mouth descended. Kit shivered and bit her lip to keep from crying out. Joshua nipped and teased, drawing each bud up tight, and Kit surrendered to the pleasurable quakes quivering through her. His fingers undid the button of her shorts, she shivered with anticipation as he slid the zipper down. Joshua trailed his fingers to her apex and, finding her warmth, he pressed his forefingers into her womanhood. Kit bucked instinctively as the pleasure ricocheted through her, and only Joshua's other hand gently covering her mouth muffled her cries.

Joshua's fingers continuously worked magic, and Kit rode him wildly, her legs quivering and shaking as the spasms began.

Kit's eyes hooded over as he slid his fingers away, yet she opened them as she heard the soft rasp of his zipper. Within moments he had withdrawn a small packet from his wallet, sheathed himself and hovered over her.

Greedily Kit pulled him down upon her, her body aching for the fulfillment that only he could provide. He hadn't removed his shirt, and he yanked it up so that his naked chest caressed her breasts. Shifting her slightly to receive him, he slid inside.

Kit exploded immediately on his first thrust. Her wanton body, pressed into the soft sand, lifted to meet him as he withdrew and thrust again. Unlike a bed, the grains of sand conformed to her, cushioning her. Adding to the intensity of the moment was the fact they were in a cabana on the beach with people walking by and perhaps stopping at any moment. When Joshua reached the summit she was there with him, and he toppled them both over into the wonderful abyss of their lovemaking. Their bodies quivered and shook together as if made to fit from the dawn of time. As the aftermath stole in, Kit opened her eyes to find Joshua looking at her. He ran a finger along her cheek.

"Mmm…"

Joshua smiled. "You look like a cat when you do that."

"Meow," Kit replied. Joshua kissed her again and then slowly he withdrew and stood up. Kit pulled her shirt down and her shorts up, but made no move to fasten her bra or redo the zipper.

Without the slightest bit of embarrassment he stood up and pulled his clothes on. "I didn't mean for this to happen," he said, moving to sit beside her again. "But in a way I'm glad. I enjoy being with you, Kit."

Kit exhaled slowly, unaware she'd been holding her breath. She desired this man, and wanting to make love with him was as essential as breathing.

Because of that, she had been terribly wanton, doing something this afternoon she had never done before. Kit, who had never made love anywhere but a bed—and that was with Joshua last night—had just voluptuously seduced a man…and in the sand where anyone could have interrupted them at any moment. While successful, her inexperience in seduction made her unsure as to how to end the moment.

Joshua picked up the book that had fallen into the

sand. He handed it to her before kissing her nose. "I need to talk to you, but my time's up. I've got to go play one more silly game. Bill about skinned my hide for skipping out early last night. For the sake of your reputation I'll slip out alone, but I'll be thinking of you every minute."

"Okay." She nodded.

He touched her nose. "When you're done reading you can find me at the pavilion if you want. But whatever happens, you are having dinner with me. My cabin at five. We'll talk then. There are some things I need to say to you, some things I want you to hear. Understand?"

Kit nodded, relief tinged with worry about what he wanted to talk about. "I understand. Dinner at five."

Joshua laughed and pressed his forefinger to her lips. Even though Kit's mouth was puffy and swollen from passionate kissing, her lips quivered with new desire. He gave her a slow grin and arched his eyebrows at her. Mirth crossed his face. "No, Kit. I said my cabin at five."

"Now who's being brazen?" she returned, a contented grin warming her face. After last night and this afternoon he still wanted her. Joshua kissed her and with a groan he strode away, leaving the flap ties loose.

As Kit watched his long lean legs carry him over the hot, pink sand, a desperate pain burned inside her. When had she fallen for him? Was there even a moment, or had her heart always known it would be this way? A black cloud appeared in the sunny sky of Kit's day.

How had she gotten herself into this predicament? Their worlds were too incompatible. He wanted a quiet, peaceful life, and she was the tabloid's baby. And then there was her father. She had no idea how he would react if she took Joshua home.

She leaned back, closed her eyes and mulled over what she had to do.

UPON HER RETURN to the ship, Kit heard the phone shrilling from all the way out in the hall. "Coming!" she yelled, more to release her frustration than for the benefit of the person on the other end. She fumbled for the pass card, worried she would miss Joshua's call. The phone was still ringing, and breathlessly she grabbed it.

"Joshua?"

"Absolutely not, Katherine Eleanor. And it's about time. I've been trying to reach you all day!"

"Hello, Father." A feeling of dread overpowered Kit, and she slumped into the chair. Her feet curled and nervously she began to twirl the phone cord as she waited for her father to begin his tirade.

He broke the silence. "How's your interview going? Getting any work done in between kisses?"

"Father," Kit protested, already knowing whatever she said would be useless. "It's not like that."

"Of course it's not, Katherine." Kit held the receiver out away from her ears and she could still hear her father shouting despite the ship-to-shore connection. "It never is with you. You've always got one excuse after another. I'm sure your mother's rolling in her grave over this latest antic. Do you really hate Blaine that much?''

"Of course not, Father." Kit bit her lip. She just didn't love Blaine as anything more than a brother, and after being in Joshua's arms she knew she never would.

"Then pack your bags. You're coming home."

"No!"

"I don't care about a story, Katherine Eleanor O'Brien! I told you I killed it. It won't get published even if you write it. Get packed. You're finished there."

Story be darned, Kit fumed. Did her father care about her or his precious reputation? "You may think I'm done, but I'm not leaving my vacation early! You can wait until I fly out at 10 a.m. tomorrow!"

"Since when did this become a vacation Katherine Eleanor?" Kit grimaced and held the phone out even farther away from her head. Whenever her father called her by her full name twice in one minute she knew she was dead.

"Katherine, did you hear me? I want you off that ship right now! Do you understand me? Now!"

"I'm not able to do that, Father." Kit tightened the phone cord around her finger, letting the tip turn bright red. "I'm on the private island. There's no way to fly home to New York. I'll see you tomorrow, okay?"

"No, that's not okay. I've got it on very good authority that you're shacking up with that…that man you claim you're interviewing!"

Kit bit her lip. Whereas her brother could sow as many oats as needed, she was to be kept under lock and key until she'd married someone acceptable—someone she didn't love.

"I'm not interviewing him."

The words rushed from her mouth, and as Kit said them she knew they were now an irreversible fact. She would never drag Joshua through the muck to spite her father. Even if she broke her heart over Joshua, at least she would retain her dignity. She was not Marilyn Roth; she was Kit O'Brien.

And Kit O'Brien did not use people for stories.

"Look, Father, I'm not writing a story. You can rest easy on that. You killed the story and it can stay dead as far as I care. Really, I ought to be thanking you. It makes my life much easier to not need anything from him but himself."

She heard her father's gasp before she continued. It was time her father respected that she was a woman who could make her own choices. "By the way, Father, if I am shacking up with him as you claim, what business is it of yours? I care about this man, and I'm twenty-eight, not eighteen!"

"Katherine Eleanor!" Kit could hear her father's roar as if she was home in New York. "This is unacceptable! You get back here and straighten this mess out with Blaine. He's been very patient with your antics, and you know your mother always hoped the two of you would wed. She's rolling in her grave, I just know it. I'll tell Blaine he can come over for dinner, and then the two of you can kiss and make up. He's a very good match for you, Kit, and I expect you—''

Kit pressed the number five button, causing a tone to come on the line. Okay, so when push came to shove she chickened out on the follow-through. ''Father, that means I've got to go. I love you! See you tomorrow!'' Quickly, before he could say anything else, she hung up.

The adrenaline rush of talking to her father gone, she slumped down on her bed and put a hand over her eyes. Great. Her father had scheduled dinner with Blaine tomorrow night. She knew Blaine wanted to marry her, but for all the wrong reasons. Joining two families was not a reason to wed. At least she could use the dinner to make that point clear. She needed to marry for love. They both did.

For one brief moment she had a vision of her walking down the aisle of the Church of St. Thomas More, and the man waiting for her at the end had been Joshua. Kit gave a short laugh and bolted up on her bed, narrowly avoiding bumping her head on the berth above.

What was the old saying about dreams being wishes your heart makes? Kit shook off that thought and set about getting ready to go home. There were bags to pack, tips to put in envelopes, and a custom declaration form to fill out before dinner.

At two minutes to five, Kit nervously smoothed down the short, knit A-line dress she was wearing and reached up to knock on the door of cabin 9134. Before her knuckles connected, the door miraculously opened.

HE'D BEEN WAITING FOR HER. He couldn't really believe it himself, but he'd been pacing like a schoolboy about to go on his first date.

After their spontaneous combustion on the beach, he'd thought of nothing else but Kit's arrival to his cabin. Tonight, more than anything, he found himself wanting everything about their last night on the ship to be perfect.

"Right on time. Come in." Joshua held the door open, and he heard her sharp intake of breath as she stepped into the room.

The room didn't look much different from the previous night, except for the large bouquet of fresh roses he'd ordered. The bright red blooms took up most of the small dining table. "For you."

"For me?" She smiled, awed that he would order flowers. "How did you manage?"

"Ah, it's amazing what I can do." His heart palpitated. He'd done it, pleased her. So far so good. "I've ordered dinner for seven. I thought that would give us time to talk."

"All right," Kit said. She moved over to him, as if wanting to kiss him.

Joshua smiled back at her, but stepped just out of reach. She pouted. "Nope, not yet. I've got this whole evening planned out, so you'll just have to trust me."

Kit's eyes widened. "Of course I trust you. I know you would never intentionally hurt me."

At her words Joshua did a double-take. Her tone had been so sincere, and her green eyes so innocent, so devoid of any manipulation. She trusted him. Those three words hit Joshua like a blow in the solar plexus. He hadn't needed to worm trust, and then later secrecy, out of her at all. From Kit trust had just come naturally. As for never hurting her, he wished he could make her that promise.

But deep down he knew they were oil and water. Hopefully when they split it would be a painless separation. At least, he'd try to give her that.

With a groan he turned to her, as if seeking his soul mate, and he pulled her toward him.

Kit clung to him as his mouth savagely found hers, the realization of what he'd just thought making him devour her lips in his need to claim her, to possess her.

He'd just thought about seeking her as if he was seeking his soul mate. Could it be true? Could she be the soul mate he'd been looking for all his life?

He knew it could happen this fast. His half brother, Mark, had met his wife one day, and literally married Donna the next. They'd been married over ten years now. Mark had sworn he'd just known, as if a tangible Cupid's arrow had pierced his heart.

But Joshua didn't know for certain that she was his soul mate. All he knew was that he wasn't finished with his need for Kit. The fire hadn't burned out yet, and until it did he wanted her. He trailed his mouth down Kit's flesh. Her hands were in his hair, fisting the long locks before she let go to pull his polo shirt out of his trousers.

When Kit ran her hands up under the navy cloth and splayed her fingertips across his chest, his resolve to talk dissolved. It would wait. Their becoming one would not. With a low cry of possession he scooped her up into his arms and carried her to bed.

AFTERWARD Kit wanted to sigh with the glory of it all. He'd been so hard and proud and not ashamed at her perusal of his body, and she had used her senses to drink him in: his musky male aura, his smooth skin covered with soft hairs and his clean scent of soap and water after a late-afternoon shower. He was still asleep, and she studied his face, her finger itching to trace his arched eyebrows and straight nose. Not wanting to wake him she instead snuggled closer, resting against his chest so that she could hear the thump-thump regularity of his heart.

Contentment filled her, and she drifted back off into sleep.

DESPITE BEING IN DEEP SLEEP, he awoke instantly when the phone rang. He reached over to get it and grunted a *yes* before hanging it back up. "Dinner's on its way."

"I guess we should eat."

"The body does need food." He grinned as he leaned over and reached on the floor for his pants.

Dusk hadn't taken over yet, and the room still had the last vestiges of sunlight streaming through the sheers. He stood, and as he put on his trousers, he watched Kit again blink off the sleep.

She fit her name. She looked like a newborn kitten as she stretched and curled in an effort to fully awaken. The result was absolutely sexy, and it was a sight he could see forever without ever getting tired of it.

Inwardly he groaned as his arousal began again, the way his body had possessed hers fresh in his memory.

Again Kit stretched languorously as if to further tempt him. It worked, for his body wasn't too happy as he zipped his pants and shrugged into a shirt.

A discreet knock saved him from pouncing on her again.

"That's dinner," Joshua announced. "I'll get it."

"Wait!" Kit wrapped the sheet around her. "As much as I'd like to remain naked, let me get dressed. We'll never eat if I don't." She grabbed for her clothes and headed for the bathroom as the person outside the door knocked again.

"You don't have to get dressed," Joshua said, giving her a light kiss as she pushed past him. "Three times is a charm."

"I'm tempted, but I know your appetite. The food won't be hot if I don't get dressed," Kit teased, and she shut the bathroom door in his face.

Joshua was sitting at the table when Kit came out to join him. "Looks good," she said.

"I've had trouble waiting and I'll admit it—I ate a roll," he said. She playfully punched him gently on the shoulder and sat down. For the first time Joshua took delight in serving a woman food.

His woman, he mentally corrected himself, because somehow that was how he felt. He had branded her his last night, and making love over and over today had proved to him that the flame was burning hotter, not burning out. Making love to Kit was freedom in itself.

They made various small talk as they ate dinner, with Joshua feeding Kit forkfuls every now and then until she slapped his hand away with a smile, gave him a conspiratorial wink and told him she needed to feed herself or she wouldn't have any strength later.

Joshua decided to behave himself for at least a few minutes. As much as he wanted to make love to her, he wanted to get to know her—the real Kit O'Brien. He did not just want to have sex all night.

Darkness began to settle, and Joshua and Kit retired to the verandah. The boat had set sail while they slept, and the boat swished through the midnight water as it churned toward Miami.

"I have a proposition for you," Joshua began. He was uncertain as to how Kit would take his offer, but he had to make it. He couldn't let her go. He had to explore this relationship, see where it could go.

"I'm all ears," she said, and gave him a smile.

She trusted him. It felt good. Finally he had found someone he could trust in return, which was why he was going to show her something he'd never shown any other woman he'd dated.

"I have a few days before I need to be back in the city. If you're free, which I hope you are, I'd like you to go with me to Upstate New York. I want to show you my farm."

"Me?" Kit's voice squeaked.

"You." He smiled his encouragement at her, sure of his decision to risk it, even though she was a city girl and he was a country boy at heart.

"I've never taken anyone there, Kit, and I want you to go with me. It's up to you to decide, but I don't want whatever this is to end when we get to Miami. I figure that we'll get a few days of peace at my farm before we have to return to the city and let reality intrude.''

There. The words were out. He didn't know why he felt so nervous. He could tolerate rejection; his father had prepared him for that. He knew Kit needed nothing from him; she had everything. Time seemed to stop as he waited for her answer.

''I'd like that. I'd be more than happy to go.'' She held out her hand and grasped his. The strength in her grip calmed him. Everything was going to work out fine.

''Good. We can change your tickets at the airport.'' Joshua inwardly sighed. You're in deep, boy. Deep. And it felt wonderful.

KIT TOSSED THE LAST of her belongings in her carry-on. Effective immediately she was moving into Joshua's cabin for the rest of the night. Tomorrow she would leave for Upstate New York with him.

She straightened her back and stretched. When had she gotten so lucky? While she didn't know if she loved him or if he loved her, she knew that they felt something for each other. He wouldn't be taking her with him if he didn't at least have some feelings for her.

Kit's gaze fell on the express envelope she'd left out of the suitcase. ''Darn,'' she said aloud. Just what was she going to do with it? She couldn't leave the materials Eleni had sent in the trash can, not where someone might find it.

No, now that she knew how treacherous Marilyn Roth was, Kit wouldn't put it past the tabloid reporter to pay the maid for the contents of Joshua's and Kit's trash cans. It would be a safer choice to take the clippings and notes with her until she could shred them and dispose of them somewhere safe.

Kit rearranged some items and shoved the envelope into her carry-on and zipped it up. The sooner she could find a safe place to get rid of the items the better. Joshua didn't ever need to know her original intention had been to interview him.

For once, she was going to keep her mouth shut. The irony of it was that if she could share the story with her father he'd say it was about time she'd learned that lesson.

She opened the door and admitted Joshua. He raised his eyebrow as he reached for her bags. "Ready?"

"I promised Georgia we'd at least go by the lounge and say goodbye."

Joshua leaned over and kissed the tip of her nose. "Of course," he agreed. "I wouldn't have it any other way."

"Then I'm all yours."

Chapter Ten

The *Tattler,* late Sunday, Nov. 24
Mary Lynn's About the Town
Kit O'Brien Defies Father

I couldn't believe it, but I saw it with my very own two eyes! Instead of returning as planned to her massive Upper East Side apartment where she lives with her father, Kit O'Brien has run away with Joshua Parker. The steward confirmed to me that she slept in his cabin last night, and I saw both of them holding hands and kissing as they waited for the airport limo earlier this morning. I also found out that Kit changed her ticket to somewhere in Upstate New York, which is where Joshua owns a farm. Putting two and two together, there is no doubt that they plan to shack up and continue the very hot and heavy relationship they developed while on the *Island Voyager* cruise ship. Poor jilted Blaine Rourke! I have to wonder how Michael O'Brien is taking this....

When Joshua finally pulled the Chevy Tahoe into the driveway late Sunday evening, Kit's first thought was his farm looked like something from a Currier & Ives lithograph. She pressed her nose to the cold window to get a better view. For the past two hours they had been driving the roads had been clear, but a thick dusting of snow still camouflaged the fields, covering everything in a blanket of undisturbed white.

She knew instantly why he loved it. She could easily picture herself living here.

"This is beautiful," she said, taking in the picturesque red barn, the immaculate white Victorian farmhouse and the surrounding matching garages, pole-barns and outbuildings that were either red or white depending on their use. "How much is yours?"

"We've been on my property for about the past ten minutes," Joshua said. "The county road runs right through it."

He pulled up and parked the car in front of the large wraparound porch.

"The sidewalk's clear!" Kit exclaimed.

"My caretaker's very efficient. Actually I called him from the airport while you left the message with your housekeeper you weren't coming home. Besides, he said the snow stopped early yesterday, so he's had a while to get it ready."

Kit wrinkled her nose. Joshua had teased her gently about being a chicken and calling home when she knew her father was at church. Surprisingly he hadn't been insulted about her not wanting to tell her father about him. He'd just brushed it off with a comment about how he understood that fathers didn't understand.

"Anyway, Greg's a great guy, and he and his wife practically run the place. You can see their house from the upstairs windows. It's over the hill. That lane over there leads to it." Joshua pointed to a metal gate that was standing open. Kit could see the tracks in the snow where the gravel poked through.

"Well, shall we? I will warn you, though, some rooms are still under construction. But most of them are done. And, before you get too nervous, the outside structure's totally solid."

"I can't wait to see it," Kit said. She was truly eager. By bringing her here Joshua had revealed a wonderful side to his personality that she hadn't seen before and wanted to discover.

As Kit followed Joshua up the brick walk to the white farmhouse, she could see evidence of well-tended gardens beneath the blanket of frosty snow.

The porch creaked only a little when Joshua opened the front door. Kit raised her eyebrows at the fact that the door wasn't locked. Joshua smiled at her. "The only people around are Greg and his wife. He unlocked it for me probably about an hour ago."

"Oh," Kit said. She had never lived anywhere where doors were left unlocked, even for a minute.

While the three-sided porch with its huge circular columns was a sight to behold, they didn't prepare Kit for the fourteen-foot ceiling of the main floor foyer and the stone fireplace in the living room that contained actual wood logs instead of natural gas.

Joshua closed the glass-inlaid front door and gestured for Kit to sit in the living room. "I'll give you the tour after I get our bags," he told her, "but first let me get this fire going."

Hours later they were still sitting by the fire, stirring their hot apple cider with cinnamon swizzle sticks. "The apples for this came from my farm," Joshua told her. "If tomorrow's clear I'll take you around and show you all the barns, the dairy operation and the orchards."

"I'm still marveling at the view from the windows," Kit said, snuggling down closer onto his shoulder. "You can see for miles. I'm so used to looking out and seeing other buildings, my only green space being Central Park."

"You have your house," Joshua pointed out.

Kit sighed in resignation as the truth hit her. She was such a city snob. "Until I came here I thought of it as a home. This is a home. Summerset is a house, a big house with lots of room and views of water."

"I'd like to see it sometime," Joshua said, his fingers massaging her scalp. It felt wonderful. They had been sitting in front of the roaring fire for hours now, drinking nonalcoholic cider and just talking. Kit couldn't remember a more relaxing, or comfortable, evening.

She could get used to this life. Nothing to worry about, no parties to go to, no antics to perform because everyone expected it of her and her Irish temper.

Her eyelids closed for a moment, the heat warm on her face. She was wearing her only heavy sweater, the one she had packed for her return to New York

City. What she would do for clothes she hadn't figured out, but maybe she just would stay in front of the fire of this wonderful house. Maybe she could stay forever. Wouldn't that be nice?

"You didn't answer me." Joshua's lips were on her ears.

"Huh?" Kit murmured, waking slightly.

"It's okay, sleepyhead." Joshua shifted. A blast of cold air hit her as the afghan moved. "Let me get you up to bed. Just sleep. I think we're both tired, and I'd like to just hold you."

He scooped her easily into his arms. She laced her arms around his neck, and Joshua carried her up to the master bedroom and deposited her on his huge feather bed. Kit sank into it as if she was floating on a cloud. Heavenly.

A fire blazed in the bedroom fireplace, and she was vaguely aware of Joshua wrapping his arms around her a few moments later. She was, however, aware of the contentment filling her as they both fell into a deep, restful sleep.

"WE SLEPT IN OUR CLOTHES!"

"That's what exhaustion does." Joshua smiled down at her, morning sunlight flickering in behind him. He had that wonderful stubble on his jaw, and Kit traced it with her finger. He was leaning up on one elbow, looking at her. She frowned.

"You changed!" She accused suddenly, seeing that his outfit was different from the night before.

Joshua's smile lit up his whole face. "I've already been outside. Greg came up early to check and make sure we were here, and his wife made some cinnamon rolls and apple turnovers for our breakfast.''

"Those sound yummy," Kit said. "Her stew last night was delicious."

"I'm sure she'll give you the recipe if you ask."

"I can't cook," Kit admitted. She saw the surprised look cross his face. "It's true. I grew up with housekeepers and servants. Even now I'm forbidden to go in the kitchen."

"I'll have to teach you," Joshua said. "But right this minute I need to go take care of a few things, and then we'll go into town and buy you some winter clothes."

"Sounds like a plan." Kit watched him walk out of the room. She sat up and leaned back against the overstuffed pillow. Like the rest of the house, the master bedroom was filled with antiques. Joshua had kept the curtains closed, and Kit hopped out of bed and opened them. The five-window bay window at the front of the house overlooked the fields beyond, and in the drive Kit could see Joshua talking with another man, probably Greg she assumed. Both men wore heavy winter coats and looked as if they belonged in an L.L. Bean catalog.

As Greg drove off, Joshua headed toward one of the barns. She really should write her observations down. She'd forgotten to do that the whole trip, neglecting the daily journal she usually kept so diligently. She'd forgotten about it after she'd decided there would be no story. She'd get the notebook out later, the idea of a warm shower appealing more.

She had never known a day so idyllic. Joshua took

her into town, and she bought clothes, boots and a coat. Once she was properly dressed for the climate, he showed her all of his property, took her to the barns and introduced her to the foal that had been born three nights ago.

"Everything's modern and working," Joshua told her. "Even though some people may call it my hobby, at this size it's an investment. I've got people in my employ, and Greg manages everything when I'm not here. We've been in the black all the years I've owned it."

"That's quite an accomplishment," Kit said as they stomped the snow off their boots and entered the house through one of the back doors.

"I like to think so." He flipped on a light switch. At 5:00 p.m. the sun had dipped below the horizon, and the clouds moving in indicated another snowstorm on the way.

JOSHUA ROLLED OVER, having spent the morning happily snowed in with Kit.

"What's this scar?" Kit had asked last night, tracing the whitened raised flesh on his back. He hadn't needed to look to know what she meant.

"It's a long story." He had frowned and then relaxed. This was Kit, and he trusted her. He'd brought her here, and she'd taken to the farm like a duck to water. She wouldn't let him down. He could trust her.

"Hey, silly, come on. You know I have nothing but time." With her toe she tickled his foot.

So he told her.

"I'll need to start at the beginning. It's a long story, and starts with a little history lesson."

She frowned. "You sound serious."

"I am." He leaned forward and kissed her nose. "It's about my father."

"Oh." Comprehension dawned in her eyes. "You don't need to tell me."

"That's okay." He smiled at her, trusting her. "You see, Kit, unlike the American Senate, which is voted on, the Upper House of the Canadian Parliament consists of 104 ordinary senators appointed by the governor general on advice of the prime minister. I aired my father's dirty laundry, mainly me, and my public comments cost him one of those coveted jobs. He told me he never wanted to see me again, that I'd destroyed him enough."

"Oh, Joshua." Her face revealed her horror.

"I know. Even though it was years later, some press articles came at the wrong time. The articles insulted and once more made a mockery of my father, right when he was again exploring a higher office. I mean, if he couldn't control his son how could he control the country? So he became a political liability who never got the office he wanted. Instead he has had to stay *éminence grise* to keep Quebec in the federation."

"What's *éminence grise?*"

"It means that despite his power he had to stay in the background. I cost him any higher public office. His only consolation is that Canada remains unified."

Joshua took his free hand, and he traced his finger down her cheek. She shivered. "You see, all the stress I caused coupled with his work took a toll. My father had massive kidney failure a few years ago. The ironic part was it occurred the day I won the Emmy."

A silence fell, and Kit waited for him to continue. "Sometimes it takes a crisis to bring people back together. For once I didn't do anything stupid. I flew to Canada immediately and had Bill Davies accept the award. Since then my father and I have managed to come to terms and forge some sort of an understanding in these past few years."

"So he's okay?"

"His prognosis is great. He's got a functioning kidney. I gave him one of mine." And with that she'd pushed him over and made love to him again.

YES, THEY COULD POSTPONE their return to Manhattan forever, Joshua thought as he dragged himself awake the next morning. He'd done the right thing in bringing her here, he decided. He could get used to this, waking up to her every morning. He reached over to push a stray strand of red hair off her face. She was beautiful when she slept, innocent and trustworthy. There was no trace of the notorious Kit O'Brien, tabloid goddess. In fact, for the first time since he'd met her, she seemed at peace, her only brazenness being during their lovemaking.

Joshua slid quietly out of bed. As much as he'd like to spend a full day in bed with Kit, he needed to meet Greg down at the barn in about half an hour. Already the sun was up, and he had only enough time to get dressed and drink a hot cup of coffee.

About twenty minutes later Joshua made his way
to the coat closet. It was even colder than the day
before, and he wanted his subzero parka. He pushed
the other coats aside and stepped a bit farther into the
tiny space. As he did, the luggage he and Kit had
stacked there after the cruise tumbled down onto his
feet.

"I knew I should have put this away better." He
stepped back and bent down to start shifting his and
Kit's cases back into the closet again. As he reached
for his stowaway bag, he caught his foot on Kit's
carry-on. As he did the bag tilted over and a tube of
lipstick rolled out. "Come on, Kit. You could have
at least zipped the bag."

Joshua stood up, bringing the bag and the lipstick
with him. As he went to put the lipstick away he
noticed the reason the bag hadn't closed properly was
because of a large overnight envelope. The envelope,
once folded compact, had expanded into the space left
in the near empty suitcase. As Joshua pushed the envelope back down he saw his name scrawled on the
outside.

Frowning, he took the envelope out of the bag, rec-
ognizing the O'Brien Publications return address and
Kit's shipboard address. The envelope wasn't sealed,
and with a bad premonition he undid the clasp and
pulled out the contents.

And then he saw it all. The memories of his past
assaulted him like a fist to the face. In black-and-
white, some articles transcribed from Canadian news-
papers, was every sordid, ugly detail of his life. And

on one of the papers someone had written "get the family angle."

Joshua read the articles again, feeling the rejection and hurt caused by the man he'd loved, the man who'd turned him away because of one childish mistake.

He had been so close to being free from the past, free from being a celebrity who would have to live with the beast resurrecting itself and rearing its ugly head.

He shoved the clippings back into the envelope and yanked out the thin, elongated notebook also in the carry-on. A reporter's journal. Dreading what he knew he'd see, he opened it. There, in what had to be Kit's handwriting, were notes. Things he'd told her in the surrey. Things he'd shared with her.

Joshua tossed the notebook back in as if the paper itself had singed him. He'd trusted Kit O'Brien.

How wrong he'd been.

Foolish man that he was, he'd told her things he'd shared with no other person. Joshua cursed himself aloud. He had thought she was different, but she was just as bad as Marilyn, maybe even worse. Marilyn hadn't pretended to care.

Joshua slammed the closet door closed. He'd given with his heart. He'd opened up to Kit O'Brien in a way he'd never opened up to anyone. What had he been thinking? Why had he trusted her? He didn't love her. He'd wanted to see where the relationship led, and he'd found out.

It went to hell.

And to think he'd thought that she didn't need anything from him. But she did. She'd lied. She didn't want him, not for himself; she wanted him for a story. Hadn't he thought Once Bitten Twice Shy at the start of the cruise? Sure, he'd been there, done that, and now, blockhead that he was, he'd done it again.

Kit O'Brien was no better than anyone else he'd ever known. Except this time he'd let the beast's master into his heart. He'd trusted Kit, actually considered taking their romance into the future as far as it would go. No, he was a fool. A bloody fool who had just been betrayed and left out to dry.

WITH A SIGH Kit rolled over and got out of bed. No matter how much she wanted to put off leaving the farm, today she needed to talk to Joshua about Thanksgiving. She'd never missed the holiday with her family, and it was probably time to make amends. Hopefully Joshua would want to meet her family. She couldn't imagine going without him.

She hadn't phoned her father again, but she knew he expected her home in time for dinner. If she brought Joshua home, perhaps her father would recognize that he, not Blaine, was the man in her life, the man she loved.

The man she loved. She flushed at that thought. She wasn't certain when she'd known for sure, but just as certain as more snow would fall later today, she knew she loved Joshua Parker with all her heart.

Maybe it had been the way he cared for his animals that had been the catalyst for her love to fully bloom. Maybe it had been the way he'd opened up to her about his past. Maybe it was the way she felt complete with him, somehow whole. She didn't know what caused a person to fall in love. Maybe all the factors just came together like some cosmic force destined to awaken her into what love was.

Whatever it was, she knew in her heart that she loved him, and no matter how scared she was to admit it, she needed to tell him how she felt. Maybe he didn't love her back, but she had to tell him and then ask him to accompany her to her family's Thanksgiving. She showered and dressed, knowing that Joshua would be out in the barns for most of the morning.

Therefore it surprised her that he was putting logs on the fire when she came downstairs.

A romantic fire, a woman in love. Ah, the possibilities. She strode forward and then froze. Something was wrong. She could sense it, see it in the way his shoulders hunched with tension. He turned to face her, and despite the fact that his expression was a mask of neutrality she knew something had happened.

"Joshua?" She spoke his name hesitantly. "I thought you had to be in the barns this morning."

"Something came up." He turned his back on her and looked at the fire for a moment. Silence blanketed the room.

Dread filled her. Had someone died? Had an animal been injured? "Is everything okay?"

"It will be." He turned back around. An icy aura surrounded him, and Kit's stomach felt full of trapped butterflies. "You might want to pack. We'll need to leave in an hour if we're to beat the incoming cold front. I'd like to get you home before it gets too late."

"I don't understand." Kit walked to the sofa and

sat down with a thump. She pulled the afghan over her. Despite the fire, the room had a decided chill.

"I'm sure Daddy wants you home for Thanksgiving."

Kit didn't understand his frigid tone. Gone was the warmth she'd been accustomed to these past few days. "Well, yes. But I was hoping that you would be coming with me. In fact, I'd planned on inviting you to meet my family. I want them to meet you."

He didn't seem too overjoyed at her announcement, and Kit's fear accelerated. "Still looking for a rise out of good old Dad, huh, Kit? Bring home the lover before you marry the acceptable guy, right?"

"What are you talking about?" Kit bristled. Somehow she was losing whatever this battle was. She wanted to fight it, but she didn't know who or what she was fighting against.

"Oh, I was just confirming your motives. And here I thought you were different."

"Look, speak clearly. What is going on?"

"What's going on?" His brown eyes blazed dark in fury as he whirled to face her. "Are you really this self-centered?"

Kit paled, but she was paralyzed under his verbal assault. What was he talking about?

"No answer." He raised one eyebrow. "At least you didn't defend yourself. I can't stomach your lies and excuses."

"Lies? Excuses?" Kit stammered.

"Your using me? Ring any bells yet? I hope I was good in bed. Your fiancé will be grateful he won't have to teach you much."

Kit struggled for her composure. Her hands shook. In two minutes he had tarnished everything they had stood for. Outraged, she leaped to her feet. "I am not using you!"

"Really?" Joshua's lips thinned to a line. "I don't believe you. No, you're no better than any other woman. Always wanting something."

"All I wanted was for us to be together."

"When? Before or after the news article you were planning to write? My secret escapade with Joshua Parker, complete with a trip to his farm. Cover material, I'm sure. At least, that's what the letter from your editor said."

Kit sank back down to the sofa as if her knees had given out. In slow motion she watched him pull the overnight envelope and the notebook off the bookshelf.

It was a battle she couldn't win, but she had to try. So much for her plan to shred the contents the moment she returned home. "How did you get that?"

"I knocked over the suitcases getting a coat. You lost some lipstick, and when I went to put it back I couldn't help seeing this." Angrily Joshua tossed the envelope onto the sofa by Kit. Some of the clippings fluttered out, the notebook opened, and papers fanned out in various angles. She made no attempt to pick them up.

Instead she watched as Joshua finished pacing and stopped to lean against the wall. His face was ice-cold. "So, no explanation?"

"It's not like that."

"Is that the best you can do?" Words brittle, he

gave a short laugh and his brown eyes narrowed. "I want to hear you admit it. You were sent on this cruise to interview me."

"Yes. I took the assignment to escape my father. He was pretty livid. Blaine is his godson."

"Your fiancé."

"He thinks he is." How could she deny it? Blaine did think they were engaged, although she'd told him no way in hell. But her father had told him yes, and in Blaine's mind it was still the dark ages when fathers decided for their daughters. When Blaine had refused to accept her refusal, she'd sent Meaty Choice down his tux.

"But I didn't know who you were on the plane. I didn't even know you were my assignment until the next morning.

"I see." Joshua nodded curtly as he took a seat in a chair across from her. His face grew impassive, and he clasped both hands in his lap and leaned toward her. "But you needed one last, or one first, fling."

"No!" Kit shrieked the denial. "I did not sleep with you for those reasons! I slept with you be-cause—" Her voice faltered and she felt silent. She would not tell him she loved him, that she probably had even back then. She would salvage at least that much of her pride.

"Because you needed to get close to me," Joshua said into the silence she'd left. "Since I was so smit-ten with you it was the easiest way to do it. And we sure had chemistry, didn't we?" His laugh sounded hollow, and a log crackled and spit on the fire.

"Absolutely not! I am not Marilyn Roth, or Mary

Lynn or whatever she feels like calling herself. Unlike her, I didn't sleep with you to get a story!''

"I never slept with her!" Joshua let loose a curse. "I make it a habit of never dating or sleeping with reporters. But you got around that, didn't you, Carol Jones? All this for your own byline?''

"For your information I'll never get my own byline. My father's probably already fired me. No, Joshua, I came here because, like you, I didn't want us to end.''

"Well, it's too late now. This relationship is finished." Joshua's tone was flat.

Kit closed her eyes. She had to fight—fight for this man. This man, who, despite this horrible situation, was the man she still loved with all her heart and soul. "No, Joshua. We aren't finished. I refuse to let it end like this. Not with you believing I'm a cheap hussy out for a story. That's not what I am. That's not who I am.''

"Maybe not, Kit. But what you are is a spoiled brat who does everything she wants with no concern for anyone else. Daddy always forgives you. Well, do you want the ugly truth? Life isn't like that.''

Kit clenched her fists as her Irish temper flared. She had to make him listen to her. He'd told her about his father, and she understood. She knew his pain, saw it almost as her own. If he could only believe that. "For your information those are my editor's notes. I was totally surprised when I found out. Here I was, hung over and having dreamed of you all night, discovering I was supposed to interview you? But after the day we spent together, I decided not to go through with it. Your personal life is just that, personal.''

''Ah, but it isn't. Wouldn't you think making love to me makes you a part of my personal life? In my book, that makes you no better than Marilyn Roth.''

Kit fought to keep the tears back. Every word he threw at her stung. Joshua paced.

''I'm sorry. I was wrong. I should have told you in the beginning about the story, and that I'd chosen not to do it.''

Joshua spun to look at her. His eyes reflected the depths of despair. She wondered if he could forgive her, but she knew she had to make him try. She couldn't let his stubborn pride, or hers, kill something so wonderful.

''I've never admitted that I was wrong before, not even after any of my antics, but I am. I'm sorry Joshua. I didn't mean to deceive you. I wanted to tell you but I didn't know how. So I tried to bury it under the carpet.''

The large room seemed oppressive and dark, and Kit watched him process her apology. He visibly calmed down, and he reached up and massaged the back of his neck as if to relieve the tension. When he spoke his voice still reflected pain.

''Look, the trash Marilyn printed destroyed the last shred of relationship I had with my father. It was the proverbial straw that broke the camel's back, and I spent years repairing the relationship. Surely you can understand a precarious relationship with one's father.'' Joshua whirled. ''Why I am doing this? I don't need to rehash this, especially with you. Go get packed. We're leaving.''

With that he strode out of the room, and Kit heard the front door slam. The ensuing quiet was deafening, and Kit slowly sank back down to sit on the sofa and let the tears flow. They carved wet paths down her cheekbones as her heart broke. She'd really screwed up. For the first time in her life she'd found what she wanted, and she'd screwed it up. She lifted her head from her hands, seeing the clippings.

Damn her for keeping the clippings and not destroying them on the ship. By keeping her secret she'd ruined the best thing that had ever happened to her.

Slowly Kit gathered the clippings and the loose-leaf paper and took the pile to the fireplace. She derived little satisfaction in wadding the papers up and watching the offending pieces burn. The fire ate them, flaring as if it was mocking her. The papers and clippings fluttered and then curled and burned. The logs hissed and popped, and the notebook smoldered to ash. But Kit knew it still didn't matter. Time had run out.

She shivered as she went to the window and looked outside. He stood there, watching one of the horses that was out for a bit of exercise.

As he gripped the railing, she could see the pride, the defensiveness etched in the hard line of his jawbone, a line that she knew could be so soft and tender when covered by her feather kisses. A light breeze lifted his long locks gently, and her heart shattered even further. She turned and went upstairs to pack.

WHEN HE RETURNED, her suitcases waited by the door. His hair had been whipped about in the cold breeze, and he shuddered. At least she had the common sense to stay out of his sight. At the shrill of the doorbell he turned. He'd told Greg to come up to the house after he put the horse away.

"Forget your key, or just being careful?" Joshua opened the front door, but the man standing in front of him wasn't Greg.

"Joshua Parker?" The man's cold expression conveyed nothing.

"Yes." Joshua frowned as he took in the oddly familiar young man who wore a heavy overcoat like those seen on Wall Street. "May I help you?"

"Blaine Rourke, and yes you can. Cameron O'Brien said Kit is here. I've come to take her home."

"You've what?" Joshua's stomach clenched as he recognized the dog food man. What ironic timing. He bristled as Blaine gazed past the door.

"I can explain, but I'd like to step inside. It's cold out here and you're letting all your heat out."

The argument was logical, so Joshua kept his conflicting emotions controlled as he stepped aside to allow the taller man to enter the room. Blaine Rourke didn't need to know what had transpired earlier in the day, that Joshua and Kit were through. Male pride dictated that Joshua didn't want the guy to have any satisfaction. "I'll give you two minutes."

"Fine." Blaine Rourke entered Joshua's foyer as if the world was built to serve him. From the way Blaine surveyed the living room and foyer, Joshua knew Blaine recognized Kit's suitcases. Blaine turned back to Joshua, his face a mask.

"Let me get right to the point, Parker, Kit needs to go home because her father has had a heart attack. One look at the clippings of the two of you together and he was on his way to the hospital with the EMTs."

Joshua clenched his fist. He refused to let Blaine blame Kit for her father's health. "Get real. Clippings don't cause heart attacks."

"Maybe not, but they probably added to her father's stress. Look, I don't have time for this. Kit is very dear to me. We've known each other since we were toddlers, and despite anything you may have seen in the papers, Kit could never offend me. I'd forgive anything she does."

Blaine's gaze flickered over the room. "I'll make no bones about it. For as long as our families have known each other they've wanted us to marry. Since Kit belongs with her family, I'm here to take my fiancée home. You are not welcome to join her."

Bile rose in Joshua's throat. Never before had he felt the urge to hit anyone, but after Blaine's condescending announcement he sure wanted to. Kit's father had suffered a heart attack. History was repeating itself. Bitterness rose in Joshua. He could have saved Kit, saved her from the pain she was about to go through. He'd been there. If only she'd wanted saving.

No, the only thing she'd wanted was her exclusive story. Joshua gazed at Blaine, his anger at Kit's betrayal finding a target. If Blaine had been able to keep

Kit controlled, she never would have erupted into Joshua's life and turned it upside down. His pent-up anger focused on Blaine, and the only reason Joshua didn't plow his fist through Blaine's nose was that at that moment Greg came through from the kitchen. "Hey, boss. Cindy's sent you some croissants and muffins for the trip back to the city. She says it's better than fast food. She's even got a thermos of hot chocolate...." His voice trailed off. "Sorry, boss. Didn't know you and Kit had company."

"Blaine Rourke."

Greg stood there with a confused look on his face, and Joshua could hardly blame him. A thumping on the back stairs alerted him to another presence. Kit.

"I'm ready. Where are you?"

Joshua heard Kit go to the kitchen, then he heard each successive footstep get louder as she came into the living room.

"Joshua?" Kit's gaze moved from him, and her green eyes widened at the sight of the other man. "Blaine? What are you doing here?"

Come on, fiancé, tell her, Joshua thought as Greg backtracked to the kitchen.

"Blaine, of course," Kit continued. "You've been sent here because of the *Tattler* blurbs. I should have known. Were they bad this week? We don't get that rag out here."

Blaine looked at Kit. "I've got a plane waiting and a car with a professional driver outside. We need to get going. The weather reports indicate there's an ice storm headed this way, and we don't need to get grounded in this godforsaken place."

"You came all the way here because of some bad press? Blaine, this is ridiculous! I'm sorry about dumping dog food over you, but you announced we were engaged without my consent!"

"Kit," Blaine said.

She wouldn't let him speak. "I'm sure whatever was in the *Tattler* couldn't have been worse than what they print about Cameron. Good God, he's got more notches on his bedpost than a beaver dam."

"I've been sent to fetch you home, Kit. Hurry, time is of the essence."

"So the press clippings about me are bad enough you had to come?"

"Although this has to be your worst antic yet—" Blaine made a slight gesture indicating Joshua "—the press is not why I'm here. I'll tell you when you're seated on the way home."

Kit's anger blazed as she slipped her feet into her shoes. "Is my father that determined to keep us together, or are you trying to save your precious reputation? I told you I am not marrying you! We aren't engaged, nor will we ever be."

A wave of relief washed over Joshua upon hearing Kit's words. She wasn't marrying Blaine. Joshua felt a little better that at least she hadn't lied to him about that. But she had lied. And she had used him. And now she needed to go home. Her father needed her. She needed to know now, not on the way home like the idiot so-called fiancé planned.

"Kit." At his gentle tone she turned toward him, hope evident. He hated what he had to tell her. "Kit, you need to go. Your father's had a heart attack."

"My father? Heart attack?" Kit's voice cracked. She bit her lip. When Joshua and Blaine both gave nods of confirmation, she realized this wasn't someone's idea of a sick joke. She turned to Blaine in absolute horror and flung herself into his arms. "No! Not my father!"

"The company plane is at the airport. Come on, Kit, time is of the essence. It's already been too long. Cameron's been at the hospital since late last night. I got delayed by the weather."

"Since late last night? Is he okay?" Guilt ripped through her. She should have been home. She should never have come to this place. Tears cascaded down her face. What had she done?

"He's in ICU. Come on, Kit. You need to be there." Blaine adjusted his arm around her and he began easing her sobbing form out of the door.

She started to turn, but Blaine somehow sensed that, and he draped his coat over her. Without a word of goodbye, Blaine took her arm and guided her away, the door of the beautiful farmhouse closing with an ominous click.

Chapter Eleven

As I reported yesterday, Blaine Rourke retrieved Kit O'Brien from her escapade at Joshua Parker's farmhouse. The wayward waif spent Thanksgiving in her father's hospital room, where he is recovering from a minor heart attack.

Rourke confirmed to me that he and Kit have reconciled, and he stood by her side when she appeared briefly and addressed the press regarding her father's condition.

When asked for a wedding date, Kit replied that her nuptials would be scheduled when her father recovers. So, readers, it seems as though Kit's father finally got his wish. Unfortunately, it took a heart attack to make Kit see reason, but at least we can finally look for a white wedding soon! Oh well, live and learn, Joshua....

Joshua tossed the paper aside and slammed his fist down on the kitchen table.

"Hey, don't hurt the table. It's innocent."

Joshua glanced up at his sister-in-law, Donna. She stood behind him in an oversize fluffy pink bathrobe. "Mark will be out in a moment. I'm making coffee. Want some?"

What he wanted was a long, stiff drink to make the nightmare that was his life go away. He pushed that thought aside. "Coffee sounds great."

"Good." Donna smiled at him, and Joshua shook his head. His half brother had probably found the one woman in the world worth falling in love with and marrying.

"He's still eaten up inside," he heard Donna whisper as Mark entered the large kitchen.

"It'll take a while," Mark whispered back.

"I can hear you," Joshua informed them. "And I'm over her."

"Sure you are." Mark nodded, disbelief evident. "That's why you're here instead of going home last night like the rest of the family did."

"My car's snowed under," Joshua replied. But he didn't buy his own excuse any more than Mark did. Especially since Joshua had taken the subway to Mark and Donna's co-op.

He sighed as the hot mug Donna handed him warmed his fingers. She plopped down in the seat next to him and put her forefinger under the edge of the newsprint. "I see you bought that rag again."

"I wanted to see what Mary Lynn had to say."

"Hmm," Donna said. She scanned the article and

tossed the paper in the waste can. "Don't tell me you believe her lies."

"I wish that's what they were."

"Oh, come on, now." Donna tapped her nails on the tabletop. "This woman couldn't print the truth if it slapped her in the face. You don't believe Kit's actually marrying this guy do you?"

"I saw them together."

Donna tossed her head, her blue eyes rolling heavenward for a moment. "You saw them when he came to tell her about her father. It was logical he came to pick her up. Next of kin always stay at the hospital. Cameron's father needed him."

"You're forgetting she betrayed me," Joshua said. He stood and paced the kitchen. Mark snagged the seat he'd vacated. "I told you what she did. I told you about the article, the clippings. She used me."

Donna tossed her hands in the air. "Men are so dense!"

Mark shrugged. "Look," Donna continued, "you need to assess how you feel about her. Obviously, you care or you wouldn't be here, dreading your empty apartment."

That was true. He'd hated the past couple of nights. Even though he was in his city apartment, somewhere Kit had never been, he could still feel her imprint next to his skin. She'd curled up next to him when they'd slept, and since their argument and her departure, Joshua hadn't known a night's peace.

He'd hated the mornings even more, for that was when he would wake up alone, without the presence of the woman he loved.

"Oh, hell." He yanked at his long hair. Today he was getting it cut.

"I see a lightbulb above your head." Donna smiled sagely. "Spill the revelation."

"I love her." Joshua paced again after making that admission. "And it hurts like hell."

Mark's eyebrows arched, and his jaw dropped slightly.

Donna, however, looked satisfied. "Ah, so now we're getting somewhere."

"You had to marry a psychologist didn't you?" Joshua accused his brother. Mark shrugged apologetically.

"Yes, he did," Donna said, "and you're glad of it. Now, dear Josh, tell me. What do you want to do about these feelings?"

"Get over them," he snarled.

Donna made a tsk-ing noise. "Come on, Joshua. Be honest with yourself. Your pride's been hurt, but aside from that, how do you feel?"

"I don't know." Stubborn pride held him. He twisted a lock of his hair around his finger and pulled on it. The pain was nothing compared to that in his heart.

When had he fallen in love with Kit O'Brien? Could he even put his finger on the date? Damn! Why did he have to fall for a woman who'd betrayed him?

And, since he loved her, did her betrayal even really matter? He hurt *without* her more than she'd hurt him.

"You know," Donna said. "You need to find out the truth."

"How?" He snapped at that easy answer. "I just dial her up on the phone, and say, 'Hi, Kit, let's get back together?' Absolutely not. She's engaged to someone else. I'm not going to interfere."

Donna took a long sip of coffee. She smiled at Joshua. "I didn't mean you."

Joshua's brow furrowed, and Mark's head shot up from the article in the *Wall Street Journal* that he was reading. "What?" Mark asked.

Donna smiled at Mark. "You, my dear husband, are going to save Josh's sorry hide. Don't you know Cameron O'Brien?"

"We've had some business dealings, yes." Mark's tone was hesitant.

"That settles it." Donna leaned back, triumphant. "Call him. We're going to get this matter settled once and for all."

Mark looked unhappy. "What do you mean we?"

Donna beamed at her husband. "It'll be our Christmas present to Josh. And think of how your mother will feel if we get him married."

"I'm not getting married," Joshua protested. Donna simply gave him a sharp glance, and he fell quiet. Just what was he going to do with the woman he loved? Shack up with her?

No, Donna was right, but male pride dictated that he didn't like being forced by his sister-in-law to see the light where Kit was concerned.

When Donna was certain his protest had ended, she continued. "Think of how your mother will stop fretting, Mark. So, like I was going to say before I was interrupted, I do mean *we,* darling husband of mine."

Mark grinned and shook his head. "It's the day after Thanksgiving. He's probably not in the office today."

Donna looked down her nose at her husband. "Since when did that ever stop the Wizard of Wall Street? I'm sure Cameron has a home number, doesn't he?"

Mark shoved the chair back and rose. "Yes dear," he said with a grin. "But this'll cost you later."

Donna drew a hand through her blond hair as her husband left the room. She turned to Joshua. "Now get yourself home and get cleaned up, you bum. We have work to do. As soon as I know some information I'll call you."

"Work?" He had to admit he was still confused by the exchange he'd just witnessed.

"Yes, work. We're going to find out the truth and come up with a plan. You love her, right?"

His silence was the confirmation she needed. "Then that settles it."

Chapter Twelve

The *Tattler*, Friday, Dec. 13
Mary Lynn's Around the Town
O'Brien Patriarch Retires

It's official, boy wonder Cameron O'Brien has taken over the helm of O'Brien Publications. Cameron, consistently called New York City's most eligible bachelor, received the board of directors' nod of approval during a unanimous vote. One of Cameron's first acts of business will be to calm wary investors. The vote came just two weeks after his father's heart attack. Doctors say the prognosis for O'Brien Publications' patriarch, Michael O'Brien, is excellent. He is expected to make a speedy and full recovery. Michael's heart attack came after his daughter, Kit, refused to return home and instead ran away and played house with Joshua Parker, writer for *Last Frontier,* the television series that ended last Friday.

Speaking of the home front, Kit has been a no-show at all the charity events she had committed to attend. Word has it that she's still smarting from the accidentally released O'Brien internal memo that exposed her as Carol Jones and said that O'Brien will no longer publish Carol Jones stories.

So Kit's prognosis isn't great. Not only did her father fire her from her job, but like the poor little plaything she is, Kit's been discarded by all her beaus. Joshua's been busy around the town on the arm of another female. Poor Kit. Just why did her lover ditch the goddess of the tabloids? Did her antics become unlivable, or did he just tire of her childish ways and wise up?

Even Kit's ex-fiancé, Blaine Rourke, has hit the road, as he was seen kissing supermodel Tara Lynwood (photo page one) at last night's opera. As for lonely Kit, she's not been seen about the town since her father's heart attack. Sources tell me that her father is disappointed in his wayward waif and is keeping her under tight wraps. One can only hope so, or her antics will send Michael to an early grave.

Cameron O'Brien tossed the *Tattler* aside. He didn't give a hoot what Mary Lynn said. The sooner he found a way to get rid of her the better. Considering he didn't own the *Tattler* he'd have to put some thought into it. But he knew it could be done. He'd take care of it right after he solved the more pressing problem of what to do about his sister.

He turned back to the man seated in front of him.

He'd grown quite fond of Joshua Parker in the time they'd been conspiring. And one thing Cameron knew for certain, Joshua was Kit's perfect match.

"I know you're frustrated. Just trust me. She should show up tomorrow night. I'm going to personally escort her. If not, then you have my permission to break the door down. My dad's heart is fine, and I'll warn him beforehand."

Joshua rose to his feet. "Thanks."

"No. Thank you," Cameron said honestly. He walked around his office desk and stood in front of Joshua. "You've played this by my rules, and for that I'm grateful. She's been miserable, but my father's health was of the utmost importance. Now, like me, he wants to see Kit happy."

"I understand," Joshua said. He did. After his own father's kidney transplant, Joshua knew firsthand how much a person's recovery depended on the people around them and the lack of stress in their lives.

Joshua closed his eyes for a nanosecond. He'd been miserable the past two weeks even though he knew Kit wasn't marrying Blaine Rourke, nor had she ever been going to.

But now, after all this time, he wasn't sure how she felt. Did she love him? Would she forgive him? On Cameron's orders Joshua had not attempted to contact Kit except for trying to connect with her at various charity events. She'd been a no-show.

Cameron reached out and shook Joshua's hand. One blond hair fell in Cameron's eye and he pushed it back. "You just make my sister happy."

No truer words had ever left Joshua's lips. "I'll die trying."

"THAT'LL BE $2,000."

Kit groaned. "I can't believe I landed on Board-walk! Again!"

"Well, your mother always said you were going to have expensive tastes." Michael O'Brien leaned forward and put his gnarled hand out. "Pay up."

"I think you've won," Kit admitted, handing over her last three hundred dollars. "Everything else I have is mortgaged. I don't know how you get so lucky."

"Luck of the Irish, my dear. I was simply born with it." Michael chuckled, and Kit reached over to pour him a glass of water.

"Well, I wish it would rub off on me. You would think I had crossed a leprechaun or something." Kit handed her father the cup. After almost two and a half weeks he was doing much better. Already he was at home, and driving his twenty-four-hour-care nurses up the wall.

Despite the leaked memo to the contrary, her father hadn't fired her. Hence Kit had taken an extended leave from her job, leaving Cameron to run the family enterprise while she assisted in the daily care of her father. Ironically she was doing what her father had wanted in the first place. She was staying home.

Despite the dire circumstances causing the situation, helping her father recover had been rather fun. Daily they had played games, read books and, most important, they had talked for the first time in their lives.

''You're thinking about him again, aren't you?'' Her father's voice cut through the silence.

Kit looked up sharply and shook her head. ''Actually, no. I was thinking about us.''

''Us?'' Her father raised one bushy gray eyebrow and began to put the Monopoly pieces back in the box.

''Yeah, us.'' Kit bit her lip and nodded. ''I've actually enjoyed getting to know the real you.''

''You found out I'm not so bad after all, eh?'' Michael gave her a sad smile. ''No, I understand what you're saying, Katherine. I've always been away. Your mother used to tell me that you acted up to get my attention.''

''I've been thinking about that, too,'' Kit admitted. She picked up the lid to the game and put it on the box. ''I think I subconsciously wanted your attention, even when it was negative. And I got a lot more attention if I acted up.''

''You've always been my baby girl.'' Her father looked wistful. ''I only wanted what was best for you, and my pride dictated that I and I alone knew what it was. But maybe it's time that I let you grow up and make your own decisions.''

''I have to sometime.'' Kit reached out and put her hand on top of her father's. ''You can't keep protecting me from the world. You've done a great job raising me. I'll be okay.''

''Is that your way of telling me that you don't want to marry Blaine?'' Her father smiled gently.

''I never wanted to marry Blaine. I don't love

Blaine, and I never have, not like that. He's more like a brother to me.''

The room grew silent, and the nurse entered. After the nurse declared her father's blood pressure was in the desired range, Kit exhaled slowly. She had lost her mother, and she wasn't ready to lose her father. She loved the old curmudgeon.

She glanced back over at her father, now reclining on his bed, the rolling table pushed away. He was waiting expectantly for her.

"So, tell me. Do you love him?"

"Who?" Kit asked.

"The man you met on the cruise ship. The one you ran off with. Joshua Parker."

Kit hesitated. Admitting the truth might stop the hurt inside her heart. "Yes, but he doesn't love me."

"How do you know?" Her father's gaze was shrewd, and Kit looked away and picked at the bedspread.

"We had a big fight before I left, he hasn't called, and I've seen him pictured with another woman." The words came out in a rush.

"So you've decided to go on with your life."

"Yes." Kit nodded. "I tried to call him a few times, but there wasn't any answer. Probably for the best. Once he told me I was a city girl to his country boy. Opposites may attract, but they can't stay together, right? Time to move on."

"Well, it might help if you know when you're going back to work."

Kit looked over at her father in surprise.

"Yes," Michael said gruffly, as if the words were

difficult for him to voice. "I've given Eleni the go-ahead to start your assignments right after the New Year. I should be fine by then. I even told her to give you something with meat on it. And to let you use your own name."

"Thank you." The scope of her father's actions was unbelievable.

"Ah, thank Eleni." Michael shrugged off his contribution. "She's already hounding me about having her best reporter out of commission."

"Yeah, right," Kit teased with a short laugh. She knew her father was extremely fond of Eleni, but that wasn't the real reason for his serious change of heart. He was finally setting his daughter free.

"It gets better, you know," her father said suddenly out of the blue.

"What does?"

"The hurt. The loss. Trust me, I know. Even though I knew it was coming, losing your mother remains the blackest moment of my life. There was no way to prepare for it. But eventually the pain fades." Michael squeezed her hand, his empathy evident in his tightened features. "Just give it some time."

"Sorry to interrupt, but it's time for your medicine and for your bath, Mr. O'Brien." The day nurse entered the room, the model of brisk efficiency.

The deep moment broken, Kit laughed as her father grimaced.

"I just had a bath! How have I gotten dirty?"

"Tut, tut, Mr. O'Brien. That was days ago. Besides, doctor's orders are to be followed, not disobeyed. Now, upsy-daisy!"

"I'll come by later, Father. Thanks for the talk."

"Kit," her father called, and Kit paused in the doorway.

"Yes?"

"One more thing. You know I love you, don't you? I know I haven't said it lately, but..." As his words faded, Kit smiled at her father. In his bed he looked so ordinary. So human. Just a frail man who had finally recognized his priorities had been wrong, just as she recognized hers had been. He was her father, and despite their occasional differences, she loved him. "I've always known, Father, but thanks for telling me. I love you, too. Have a good bath now, okay?"

With the first contentment she'd felt since hearing the news about her father's heart attack, Kit left the room.

"So, KIT, that's your mystery man." In the evening shadows Cameron's voice was low, but his mirth was unmistakable as she came downstairs. "Quite an interesting story about *Last Frontier* in *Television Today,* wouldn't you agree?"

Tossing aside the magazine that arrived earlier, Cameron dropped two ice cubes into a tumbler and poured himself a straight scotch. Kit watched as her older brother eased his lean frame back into the overstuffed blue-striped chair that had been some designer's whimsy. He took a long swallow before setting the glass down and pulling out a cigarette.

"Cameron!" Kit coughed as Cameron lit the cigarette and exhaled slowly. Her irritated glare didn't affect her brother. Four years older, Cameron had always considered himself far superior to her. Well-manicured fingers flicked the ash into the crystal receptacle, and he shot Kit a bemused look.

"The apartment will air out, Kit. That's why we've got these two-story ceilings, anyway."

"Father would have your hide if he knew you were smoking in the house," she argued, her hands making a fist in the designer slacks she wore. "He thought you quit."

"I had, up until his heart attack. Besides, his room is on the other end of the apartment." Cameron waved a hand toward the second-floor loft area and the smoke drifted lazily upward. "None of this smoke's going to reach him, Kit. Chill out a little. You've been nothing but nerves since your cruise."

"Well, you didn't sit at the hospital every day. I did."

"I'm not saying you aren't a martyr, sweet sister." Cameron raked his free hand through his sandy-blond hair. "Despite your childish antics you've always been the reliable one. Father wouldn't have recovered as quickly without you. I'm just saying you've been rather testy since your trip. I mean, you were press fodder for a few days, what with your so-called departure to his farm and then your brief reengagement to Blaine."

"And you thought you were the only headliner in the family," Kit retorted. She leaned back in the chair, willing herself not to think of Joshua. After her father's pep talk she felt better, and she wasn't going to let Cameron spoil her first good mood in weeks.

Cameron stubbed his cigarette out and pestered his sister with another irritating, mocking grin. "I'm going to have to shoot for some more press. I wonder if there's an actress I could hook up with. Hmm. Think Joshua might have any discards?"

Kit leaped to her feet. Normally she dished it out just as well as she got it, but this time she fought to keep back the tears.

"Oh, sit down," Cameron said. His blue eyes looked almost bored with her overblown reaction. "You know I'm just teasing you."

Instead of complying, Kit paced the huge living area of the apartment while her brother lounged. The room, with its wall of high windows and phenomenal view of Central Park, was truly magnificent, especially now that the room was decked out in every kind of red and green Christmas decoration imaginable.

She certainly didn't feel much in the Christmas spirit this year. In fact, she hadn't attended any of her typical A-list charity events of the season.

"Cat got your tongue?" Cameron lit up another cigarette and Kit realized he was staring at her. She frowned as her brother slid his legs up onto the sofa and crossed them at the ankles, his Bruno Magali loafers on the cushions.

"Oh, stop," Kit snapped bitterly. "You're still digging for what happened, aren't you? I kissed him. That's all."

Cameron raised his eyebrows in speculation. "Come on. You lived with the guy for a few days."

"Use your imagination." Kit was extremely testy

now. She held up her empty water glass, and Cameron stood to instantly retrieve it. "More please."

Cameron smoothed down the cuff of his sleeve before getting Kit more ice water. "I just wanted to make sure of how you felt."

"Dumped. He's been pictured with another woman, and it's past time I move on with my life. Happy now? You know, maybe I can be the most eligible bachelorette. What do you think? Do you think I have a chance? Will I get my own mail carrier?"

"Ooh, ouch. You're testy." Cameron rolled his blue eyes, and Kit knew she hadn't really offended him at all.

She shot him a steely look and stood up, forgoing the cold drink. "I'm going to get ready. I still can't believe you're dragging me to this awful charity dinner and auction."

"It's our charity and I needed a good-looking woman on my arm. And since I'm such a swinging bachelor, you should be honored."

"Gee, thanks. You just needed someone who won't get in the way of new conquests. I'm sure your hormones are getting restless, but that article should help your prospects." Even to her own ears her voice sounded unusually biting.

"Score one for Kit. Now go get ready," Cameron quipped, laughter doubling him over as she stomped off toward her room.

UPSTAIRS, Kit angrily pulled out the source of her misery and traced a finger gingerly over a newspaper clipping of Joshua. The pain grew in her chest. She was the one having the heart attack, not her father. Hers was the one breaking into millions of pieces.

The only silver lining to her father's tragedy was that for the first time in years she and her father had really communicated.

Now she just needed to get over Joshua. She tossed the clipping aside. In the past few weeks Joshua had been busy. For someone who hated press, he had garnered a lot of it.

He had attended three charity functions, his escort being a petite blonde that had hung on to his arm and smiled for the cameras. The press hadn't named her, but Kit could tell by the caring expression evident on Joshua's face that they were more than friends. One photo captured him kissing her on the cheek, his arm at her waist. There in black and white was the truth, and the truth hurt. He had easily dismissed her. It was over.

Kit angrily crumpled a clipping. Somehow she'd hoped that after he calmed down he would have come after her. Fat chance. When you wish upon a star, the star burns you.

Not once had he even called to find out how she, or her father, was. She had been discarded like yesterday's news. It hurt. It hurt like hell.

Kit bit her lip. She would not cry again. She could mend her broken heart. Then why didn't she feel convinced? She buried her face in her hands and gently pressed her head into the soothing flannel of her pillowcase. She closed her eyes in an effort to shut out

his image. Instead Joshua Parker loomed ever closer,
nearer, calling her name....

"KIT! KIT, WAKE UP!" Already dressed in his black
tuxedo and black tie, Cameron stood over his sister
and shook her shoulder roughly. His eyes had missed
absolutely nothing. Kit groggily sat up, clippings
crunching under the weight of her body.

"I'm late aren't I?" she asked simply. She tried to
roll back over. "Go without me."

"Absolutely not." Not when so much was riding
on Kit actually making an appearance. He pulled her
to a standing position and steadied her when she wobbled. "I am not going to this thing alone. Besides, I
paid $1,000 for your plate and you're going to be
there to eat it. Come on. It'll be fun. Rub the sleep
from your eyes and get moving."

He reached over and turned on the bedside light.

"The real reason comes forth," she mumbled.
"You go. They'll never miss me."

She didn't know how wrong she was. "This is our
foundation. You'll be missed." Cameron touched his
sister's cheek with his finger. Time to cajole. "The
research center was one of Mother's favorite charities.
Come on, you know we've planned this for weeks.
Besides, what would people say if you didn't show?
You've canceled every other charity event you were
to attend. People are starting to wonder. If you don't
show they'll say you eloped or, worse, that you had
a mental breakdown."

"Okay, okay." Kit stood up, a few clippings stick-
ing to her before fluttering to the floor. She glanced

at the crumpled clippings strewn on her bed. "Thanks for not saying anything."

Cameron smiled at her gently. He knew how heartbroken she was. Well, that would all end tonight. "Get moving. I'll see you in a few."

He headed downstairs and finished adjusting his bow tie in a hall mirror. Tonight's dinner auction was one of the mandatory galas of the Manhattan Christmas season and more than fifteen hundred people would be in attendance. But, of course, one was more important than the others. A ding of the private elevator let him know the nurse had brought his father down.

"So," his father's voice called across the great room as the elevator door opened, "is she going?"

"She was asleep, but she's going." Cameron strode across the room and headed toward the wrought-iron cart that held the drinks. He raked his left hand through his sandy-blond hair. "She dozed off."

"But she's going." Michael nodded his approval and then waved the nurse away. "She needs to be there. It's important, and not just because she volunteered."

"We both know why it's important," Cameron said, knowing his father referred to Joshua. "I think she's forgotten what she signed up for, but she's going, and that will work to all of our advantages." Cameron ran a well-manicured finger around the rim of an empty glass. "Tonight Kit needs to—"

"Kit needs to what?" Kit interrupted as she entered the room. She gave her father a kiss on his forehead. "Were you about to say that Kit needs to hurry?"

"Exactly," Cameron finished easily, masking his white lie with an appreciative smile for his sister's appearance. He set the glass down. "But the wait was worth it. You look stunning."

"Absolutely," her father agreed. "Your mother would be proud. You're a spitting image of her, you know."

Kit blushed. At the last moment she had debated about wearing the floor-length, white-satin gown.

"Flatterers," she teased.

"I'm glad you decided to wear that dress." Cameron surveyed his sister appreciatively. "White looks good on you. I also like the missing middle."

"Well, I'm tired of black." Kit touched the white sheer material that veiled her stomach from just below her breasts to right above her navel. The same white sheer material of the middle covered her arms from the low scooped neck to the wrists. The contrasting shiny white satin and sheer white mesh knit created an illusion effect.

"Anyway, I donated my black cruise dress to tonight's auction. It's not like anyone died, right?"

"That's for sure," her father said gruffly. "The doctor says my ticker's got quite a few years left on it. He also said that to help it along my children should stop causing me stress."

"Ohh, that's our cue to go, Kit," Cameron said with a laugh.

"Not quite yet." Michael interrupted, and Kit raised her eyebrows in speculation at her father's gruff tone. "Cameron told me what you were wearing. I had him get these out of the vault. Son?"

Cameron picked up a long black velvet box. His fingers easily revealed the one-carat solitaire earrings and a matching two-carat solitaire that was suspended on a thin, white-gold chain.

"It's your first night out in a while and I want you to look your best. These were some of your mother's favorites, remember? I got them for her on our tenth wedding anniversary, and she always said they were lucky."

Kit fought back a tear as the diamonds caught the light and made it dance. "I'd forgotten all about these."

"Yes, well they're perfect. Very understated, yet the perfect accent. Now they're yours. Help her with them."

Cameron's cool fingers removed the necklace Kit wore and replaced it with the diamond. He stepped back to survey the result as Kit removed her earrings and replaced them with the matching solitaires. Cameron looked at his father for approval.

"Perfect," Michael said with a nod. "Tonight's going to be a lucky night for you, Kit. The luck of the Irish."

"I was born on a Friday the thirteenth, Dad."

"Exactly. Time to make your own luck, Katherine. You were born with it, you know. Since today is a Friday the thirteenth, claim the day back. And I must say you look beautiful. Any man would be honored to dance with you."

Kit rolled her eyes at Cameron and smiled.

"Now, enough of this mush. I've got a date for cards with Nurse Goodbody." Michael's eyes twinkled as the young night nurse returned. "Have a good time, and, Kit, do me one last favor. Be sensible."

Kit stared after her retreating father. Sensible? Just what was that supposed to mean?

Chapter Thirteen

Kit had to admit that the evening turned out to be fun.
Even the food had been good.

"It's almost time for the auction." Eleni returned
to the table and looked approvingly at Kit's empty
dessert plate. "I'm glad you're here, Kit. You didn't
forget that you're helping out, right?"

Kit frowned. "Huh?"

"You know, there's some great stuff in here,"
Cameron interrupted, looking up from the auction catalog. "An original Doonesbury, assorted items of
clothing and jewelry from celebrities, autographed
photographs, an original Myrrh painting, and look, an
autographed *Last Frontier* script that someone named
Mark Cooper donated. Hey, Joshua Parker wrote the
episode, so it's his autograph. I'll have to buy that for
you, Kit."

"Shut up, Cameron." Kit pushed the chair back
and rose to her feet before she strangled her brother.
"What are you talking about, Eleni?"

"The auction? The stage? Like last year you're
supposed to bring the items out and so forth."

"What?" Kit didn't like the way this sounded. Why hadn't anyone reminded her? "I didn't volunteer for this."

"Look, Larry's waiting." Eleni pointed to the stage. "We've got to get this thing rolling or we'll be here all year."

"Hey, Kit, are you sure you don't want to look at the program?" Cameron held it out.

"It seems there isn't time." Kit shrugged and, white dress swishing about her legs, she followed Eleni.

Last year's auction had taken more than two hours and had raised $75,000 for the cancer research center. Over an hour later Kit's smile remained frozen on her face as she brought out each item.

Kit held the tone-on-tone rose fabric of her black dress momentarily, remembering the night that it had inspired. Well, at least it would go for a good cause, she thought bitterly. It wasn't as if she needed it anymore.

"Oh, good." Larry's voice was already beginning to announce the item as she carried it out. "Why, our hostess Kit O'Brien donated this dress. The bidding for this lovely black number will start at..."

"Five thousand if she puts it on."

"What?" Larry paused. Kit peered across the crowd and tried to get a look at the man who had spoken. He was standing near the exit, and like the other men in the room he was wearing a black tuxedo.

"I said I'll donate $5,000 to the center if she goes and puts it on." The man spoke again, louder this time, and Larry turned and gave Kit a questioning look. Still holding the black dress, Kit froze. The man's voice wasn't familiar. She willed her stomach to settle down. It wasn't Joshua, but why should he be here anyway?

"Kit, did you hear that?" Eleni was by her side in an instant. "Five thousand just for wearing the dress. Go put it on. You must!"

Kit held the silken fabric. She didn't want to put the dress on, but it was such a little gesture for $5,000, and the money would help so many. "All right." She drew her chin up. "I'll do it."

"One dress being put on, sold for $5,000," the auctioneer said cheerfully. "We'll skip this item and sell it when Kit comes back to model it for us. Our next item is the auction of our first lovely bachelorette, Lindsey Hill—"

Offstage Kit changed in the small makeshift dressing room. She glanced up as Eleni entered. "It's not Joshua, darling, so don't worry. I'm not sure who made that offer, but it wasn't him. I overheard someone say it was someone named Coop something."

"Good." Kit's shoulders sagged in a mixture of relief and disappointment. Of course Joshua wasn't here. He had no reason to be.

Sure there was a *Last Frontier* script, but he could get one of those anytime. Besides, if he wanted her, he knew where to find her. All he had to do is pick up the phone, something he obviously hadn't decided to do. No, she was like yesterday's news. Discarded.

And to think she had pined for him…thought they

might have a chance…thought he might be able to forgive her. Yeah, right. He had turned out to be as shallow a person as he had claimed her to be.

Kit clenched her fist, counted to ten and tried to relax. It didn't help. Her mind was still muddled, still processing. *I don't love him!* She angrily told herself. *I'm over him. I don't care that there had been no answer at the farm when I called, and no answering machine. I have my pride, and my pride dictates that Joshua is not in my life any longer. Three attempts to call was enough. Joshua is not worth my—*

"Eleni? What did you just say?"

"I said it's time to get back out there."

At that, Kit drew herself up and pushed all fear aside. There was one way to send a message to the world that Kit O'Brien was back, and that was not to hide out in a dressing room.

"I'm ready, Eleni. I'm going out there to sell this dress so I can go home."

Wanting to just get it over with, Kit made one final appraisal in the mirror.

"Kit, look, I don't think you realize that once out there you need to—" Eleni began.

Kit brushed Eleni's words off. "I realize I have to sell this dress before I can go home. Let's go." Ignoring Eleni's strangled attempt to finish speaking, Kit strode back onto the stage.

"Look, Kit's back with the dress on. What a gorgeous dress, wouldn't you agree, folks? And what perfect timing. You're the last item up for bid." Larry gestured with his arm, pointing directly at Kit.

Her brow furrowed and she hesitated. "Larry? What are you talking about?"

"Why, you're bachelorette number ten, Kit. In fact, why don't we just combine the dress with the date, huh? A two-for-one deal, folks."

"Excuse me, but I don't know what you're talking about."

The microphone whined, and she shuddered. Larry covered it as she approached.

"You signed up months ago to be the last bachelorette," he told her. "Don't blow this now, Kit."

He was right. She had signed up. She'd been in a snit after an argument with her father and had agreed in order to spite him.

"I changed my mind," she whispered to Larry. "Tell them that because of my father's health I must cancel."

"Can't do," Larry responded with a shrug. "You're on the block. It's in the program."

"No." Kit grated her teeth. "Absolutely not. You can sell the dress, not me."

"Kit." Kit jumped when Eleni approached.

"Eleni, I'm not doing this," she hissed. "Absolutely not. I'm done with antics."

"Hold on a moment, folks," Larry announced to the crowd before clicking the mute button on microphone. He turned to her. "Listen, Kit, if I was a regular auctioneer I would let you off the hook, but I'm not. I'm the director of your foundation, and I've known you since you were in diapers. You must do this. Think of the money it will raise. And it's only a date. Make it drinks, and you can dump the guy after a glass of wine and leave.''

Like the boy who cried wolf too many times, no one believed her now that she was serious. She didn't want to auction herself. Hearing the murmurs in the crowd, Kit knew they thought she was stalling. ''What's she up to now?'' someone asked. ''God, is she going to pull an antic?'' ''Of course,'' someone else answered. ''She always does.''

''No. Not tonight,'' Kit said to Larry and Eleni. They didn't listen.

''Sorry, Kit. You can fire me later, but you're going to do this,'' Larry said. He clicked the microphone on. ''Okay, folks. Our last item is a date with our notorious bachelorette, Kit O'Brien. And she'll even throw in the dress for free, if the price is right. Now I know there are plenty of single men out there, right?''

Larry grinned as the hoots began. ''Exactly. I knew Kit's brother couldn't be New York City's only eligible bachelor.''

Their hoots buoyed her ego, and Kit's confidence returned. Since she had to do this, at least she could get into the spirit of it. She had to prove she was back, right?

The noise died down and Kit turned on the charm for her male audience. ''As you all know, cancer research is important to me. My mother died of cancer, you know, and a date with her baby won't come cheap. That's one thing I'm not, guys, is cheap.''

"So will you be at my beck and call if I buy you, Kit?"

Kit grinned and sashayed a bit before she answered Blaine. "You'll have to pay up to see."

Blaine gave a catcall, much to the distress of the token brunette date he had sitting by his side. Kit winked at him again. He'd been great when she had explained it really was over between them.

As the room erupted in laughter and whistles, Larry rapped his gavel on the podium and began. The bidding was spirited, and Kit's shoulders sagged in relief as the bidding reached $5,000. At least she wouldn't be humiliated with a low selling price.

Down to about three gentlemen, the bidding was increasing by $500 increments. It didn't matter, Kit thought. After Joshua Parker, it didn't matter who bought her. She would never allow her heart to be hurt again.

"Ten thousand." A gasp spread through the crowd. Whoever it was stood against the very back wall. Was it the man who had made the earlier $5,000 offer to buy the dress?

Kit stared in disbelief. The man who had made the earlier bid had purchased her. But it was the person to his right that caught her attention. Someone who looked a bit like her purchaser. Someone she knew well. Intimately. Joshua.

Kit's mouth dropped open and she lost her train of thought as Larry ended the bidding. "Sold for $10,000 to number 2045."

Kit left the stage and headed for the dressing room.

She closed the door behind her and leaned against it, breathing heavily.

"Kit?" Eleni knocked on the door, and Kit let her enter. Eleni frowned. "Are you okay?"

"Sure." Kit's legs shook, and she sank into a chair. "I've just publicly prostituted myself. And in front of Joshua! Why is he here? Why won't he leave me alone?"

"Oh, Kit, please. It was very respectable and for charity. Look on the bright side. Jennifer Simons brought in eight thousand, and you topped her by two."

Kit momentarily closed her eyes. "Yes, I guess I did," she finally whispered. But she didn't add the rest of her thoughts, that Joshua probably thought being in the auction was just another of Kit's antics. He'd called her a child and a spoiled brat, and she'd just lived up to that, again. The fact that she hadn't wanted to do it, the fact that she'd changed, wouldn't be noticed by anyone.

"Huh?" Realizing Eleni had spoken, Kit inclined her head and looked at her editor.

"Kit, you really should pay more attention. I said you should be proud of yourself! Look at it this way, you've brought in much more than the dress alone would have fetched. The auction will top $100,000 tonight. I can hardly believe it myself. Anyway, get dressed and go. Whoever your gentleman is, he's paid for you and he's waiting."

"Whatever." Kit shrugged. She didn't care. All

she had cared about had been Joshua, and that was gone. He sure hadn't bid on her, had he?

She slowly changed back into her white dress, giving one last cursory look at the black dress before leaving it on a chair. She didn't want it. She adjusted her necklace, sending the diamond spinning like a star.

With determination she pasted another smile on her face. If her luck held, she wouldn't have cause to upend a water goblet on Joshua. Now that would be a worthwhile antic.

Her stomach churning, she absently patted down a wayward hair and went back out to join the party.

JOSHUA WATCHED KIT reenter the ballroom. The auction over, people mingled and took advantage of the music and lowered lights. His gaze followed her as she stopped at the open bar for a glass of wine. He could tell she didn't want it by the way she gripped the glass, as if it gave her a sense of security.

He smiled. He had to give her credit; she'd shown up and done the auction as scheduled. He took a sip of water.

Cameron had come through. She'd finally shown up at a charity event. It was about time she hadn't backed down. He was proud of her, the way she'd stood on the stage in all her glory. It had been all he could do to keep his fingers still and not bid on her himself. It had been Cameron's idea for Joshua to have a stand-in. Cameron had insisted that his sister would back out if she'd known Joshua was there.

So instead Mark had done the honors of purchasing Kit. Who would have thought his brother would have been clever enough to have her wear the dress again? Joshua fingered the glass and chuckled. When he'd seen her in the dress his heart had pounded in his chest. Memories had flooded over him. The dress was lucky. The night she wore it he'd made love to her, joining his soul to hers. He wished he'd known then what he knew now—that he truly loved her. She was the only woman for him.

He hoped she returned his feelings, and that he could convince her that together they had a future.

Yes, this plan had better work. He needed Kit, needed her back in his life. He pushed all doubt aside. It was time he and Kit both got what they deserved.

SMILE FIRMLY IN PLACE despite her inner nervousness, Kit approached the man who had bid on her.

''Ah, you are the very elusive and expensive Kit O'Brien.''

Kit forced herself to meet his gaze. He had nice eyes, but they didn't make her burn like Joshua's had. He grinned, but Kit didn't find it heartwarming. Still, because he'd paid so much she knew she should be nice, so she gave him a noncommittal smile.

''I've heard a great deal about you, Miss O'Brien. So much that you've cost me nearly $20,000 in the past two weeks. You must be some woman. It's going to be fun getting to know you.''

She frowned at his tacky choice of words. Great, her dumb move of agreeing to this bachelorette auc-

tion would now haunt her. She didn't want to partic-
ipate, but she'd see the purchase through to its com-
pletion. She regained her composure, relying on years
of outrageous behavior. Her tone low, she said,
"Whoever you are, I am more than just some woman."

He laughed. "Ah, that you definitely are. You've
managed to do something no other woman has, and
it's piqued my interest considerably, I'll tell you that.
I was hoping we'd meet soon."

What was this guy talking about, and who was he?
Kit frowned again. "Not to sound rude, but I didn't
catch your name. You are?"

"Ah, so you don't know who I am. No wonder
you didn't…" He stopped himself and shrugged. "It
doesn't matter. We'll have plenty of time in the future
to get to know each other."

Kit gave him a thin smile and set her untouched
wineglass on the table. "That remains to be seen,
uh…" She paused with a flourish and waited for him
to tell her his name.

"Darling, stop baiting her. You've played your part
well. Time for the finale," a feminine voice called.
Kit bristled as the blonde from the tabloids came up
and linked her arm through his.

Of all the nerve! The woman had been first with
Joshua and now she was with the man who purchased
her? What was going on? Who was this woman?

The man kissed the woman's cheek. "As you wish,
dear." He looked at Kit thoughtfully, his eyes warm-

ing. "I'm Mark. And this lovely lady is my darling wife, Donna."

"Flatterer," the blonde said, raising her lips for a kiss.

"Wife?" Somehow Kit managed not to falter. Inwardly every nerve ending screamed and panicked.

"It's good to finally meet you Kit," the woman said extending her hand. Somehow Kit managed to shake it. "Mark's teasing you. He's always such a joker, that's why we let him have the fun job of bidding on you."

Kit's confusion overwhelmed her. Why was Joshua fooling around with a married woman? Did her husband know about it? And why did a married man just buy her? "I don't understand."

But she knew she was about to. Her skin prickled with awareness as he approached.

"Hello, Kit. I do believe we've already met." His rich French-Canadian voice murmured into her ear, and his heated breath tickled more intimately than any lover.

Kit whirled around, surprise evident.

"Don't speak," Joshua implored, his hand already steadying her arm and stopping her flight. Expertly he began to guide her toward the dance floor.

Her body reacting to his touch like a person starved for food, Kit pasted a smile on her face as a friend of her father's waved at her.

"Great," Kit murmured. Just what she didn't need. She tried to draw away. "Would you please let me go? I'm hosting this thing."

"No, I don't think so." Joshua led her through the waltz, an amused grin crossing his face. "I do believe I bought you. I think I'll start our date here. If you don't mind."

"I mind." Kit smiled and nodded at another friend of her father's as Joshua twirled her around the floor.

"Too bad. You sold yourself, and I purchased you. A very cut-and-dry deal, considering I've waited long enough to be with you again."

Joshua readjusted his hands on Kit's back, and she trembled as her body reacted to his touch. Shivers went up her spine, and instantly she felt the heat everywhere at once. Control. She had to get control. Her body might crave his touch, but her mind knew that she couldn't allow that to happen. She wasn't over him yet, how could she ever be if she made love with him again?

"I don't think this is a good idea," Kit said with an exaggerated toss of her head. "I'm over you."

"Ah, did you go fishing?" Joshua had the audacity to chuckle.

"What?" It took Kit a moment to remember the comment he made on the ship about fish in the sea.

"You're such a darling. No wonder I've missed you." Joshua moved Kit even closer, sending more heat flaring between them. "By the way, don't you think my half brother, Mark, looks like me?"

"Half brother?" Kit whispered. Instantly it clicked. Joshua's escort to all the functions had been his sister-in-law. She remembered he had once mentioned their names.

"Half brother," Joshua confirmed. "He's a Wall Street financier and a friend of your brother's."

"How nice," Kit managed, inwardly reeling as she put it all together. She should have known her brother was behind this.

She looked at Joshua. Although he hadn't been with another woman, that didn't excuse his insolent behavior. He'd tossed her out of his life and he hadn't called.

Stop it! She chided herself, stilling the fingers that had been about to weave their way into his now shorter hair. No touching, no matter how good he looked.

His hair was away from his face, with brown waves only to the nape of his neck. Kit's breath caught in her throat. She had to get away from him. She had to regroup. She needed to be angry with him, not about to hyperventilate with desire. Having her body and brain at war was not a good thing. Inhaling, she mustered every bit of reserve she had.

"Look, Joshua, ten thousand or not, unlike on the cruise, you cannot expect to come in here and sweep me off my feet. You cannot just saunter over to me and expect me to just welcome you with open arms after what you said to me before I left. Who do you think you are?" Even her own ears detected the malice in her voice.

Joshua's features darkened, and his eyes glittered. "I'm the man who watched your conveniently forgotten fiancé show up at my door. I'm the man who read in the tabloids that you were engaged, after you'd denied it to my face. I'm the man you betrayed when you lied about a story you needed to do. And for about a week I thought I was just another of Kit O'Brien's antics to get her own way. That's who I am.''

Kit's brain reeled. She knew she had hurt him. But at the farm he hadn't wanted to listen to her apologies or trust her again. And that had hurt her, more than she would ever let him know.

''I apologized already,'' Kit snapped. ''And, as you so eloquently put it at the farm before I left, I would suggest that we don't have anything further to do with each other. It'll be best for everyone involved.''

''Perhaps it *was* best.'' Joshua stressed the past tense. He shrugged his shoulders as if the matter was of little consequence. ''But now you have an agreement to honor. Need I remind you? I paid for you. You are mine.''

Without another word Joshua swept her into the next dance. His tight hold was heaven, and as her body responded, Kit attempted to pull away. Instead Joshua tightened his grip and simply held her closer.

''Back where it all started, with a dance. Let's begin again, Kit.''

Joshua's voice sounded low and husky. His legs drifted into contact with hers, and even the layers of fabric between them could not stop the spark of desire.

''I'll give you your money back. Double.''

''I don't want money, Kit. I want you.''

His husky admission, coupled with his thighs touching hers as they danced, was too much.

Her brain reeled, her body cried yes, and her heart beat with love for him. The conflicting emotions inside her overwhelmed, and without another word Kit yanked free. Struggling for poise, she walked to her table. All she had to do was retrieve her brother so they could leave.

As she wove her way through the crowd, Cameron came into view. Inwardly she groaned. As usual, her brother already had some bimbo next to him. From where Kit stood it was obvious the two were going to make a night out of it.

"Kit." Cameron barely glanced up as she approached. "This is Emily."

"Nice to meet you," Kit replied stiffly. "Cameron, I'm ready to leave."

"Sit down, Kit." Cameron's gaze flickered over his sister, deliberately ignoring her request. "There's no hurry, is there?"

"Actually, there is. I want to leave."

"Don't run away without this." Kit whirled to find Joshua holding her dress.

"You can keep it," she shot back. "I'm not planning on ever wearing it again."

His warm breath tickled her left ear as he leaned forward and placed the dress onto her arm. "You will." His voice was measured, low. "You will wear it for me. *Très séduisante, ma chérie.*"

Kit stepped back away from him and tossed her dress on the table. How dare he! The nerve. She shoved aside the part of her that still reeled with love for him. "As I said earlier, you and I have nothing further to say to each other. Take your delusions elsewhere."

Her brother looked up briefly before returning to toy with the new bimbo's fingers. Kit fumed as Cameron refused to defend her, and she shot the traitor a dirty look.

"I'm over here." Upon hearing Joshua's silken voice, Kit's frustration began to crescendo.

"Didn't I tell you to go?"

"No, you told me that I had delusions." Joshua shrugged.

"Whatever! You know what I meant. You may think this was an antic to get your attention, but it wasn't. I committed to this auction months ago. Leave."

For a moment Joshua was tempted to do just that. He'd played by her brother's rules, waiting to come to her until the right time. Then he'd purchased her so she didn't embarrass herself, and then he'd practically declared his feelings for her while they were on the dance floor. Or at least he thought he had. Maybe he hadn't. He'd been so furious with her cold rebuke. The last thing he'd wanted, or had prepared for, was for her to tell him she didn't want him.

He took a deep breath. He wasn't going to make the mistake of turning away. He'd already made that costly error once, turning away at the farmhouse when she'd been ready to fight for their love. He knew that now. No, it was his turn to lower his pride and fight. Especially when he knew they had something special.

"Kit, it doesn't matter when you decided to sell yourself. Antic or none, I'm not leaving without you. We belong together." His eyes glittered, and Kit tried to steady her nerves.

"In your dreams. After three weeks you cannot just waltz in here and expect to pick up where we left off. I do have principles!" Her body shook, but she wasn't sure if it was with rage or desire. She still loved this man.

He smiled tenderly. "Yes, you told me that, once upon a time. But how soon you forget. What happened the last time you told someone you'd see them in your dreams?"

Damn him! Kit shuddered, losing control of her fury. Of all the egotistical things, and of course he had to be right. Joshua had haunted her dreams from the very first night. He was her paradise, and he knew it. And he stood there goading her. Baiting her with the truth.

Truth she didn't want to face.

Kit's Irish temper raged, and her hand reached out of its own volition. Whatever he was fishing for was not what he was going to get. He could not do this to her. He could not just stroll in and expect her to fawn over him. Of course she wanted him to do that, but that was beside the point. She had her pride to consider. And pride dictated what it always did.

The movement of her arm was automatic, the glass cool in her fingers despite its only being half-full.

"You know, Joshua, you need to find some other fish in the sea," she said, her arm arcing. "Why don't you go swimming for some?"

Kit heard the gasps around her as she tossed the remnants of the water goblet over him. Water splotches soaked into his tuxedo, causing a tone-on-tone polka-dot effect on the black fabric and the white pleats of his shirt. Kit raised her chin in absolute defiance.

If there was any conversation or whispers in the room, Kit didn't hear it. The other guests dropped away, faded into the background as if Kit and Joshua were the only two in the ballroom. His brown eyes had narrowed to slits, and a shiver shot through her. She faced him, ready for the final showdown.

Joshua's cheek twitched as he studied her. For being doused with water, he was oddly calm, a contrast to Kit. She clenched her fists, and her arms shook. Even angry she was the most beautiful woman he'd ever seen. With that Irish temper, being with Kit would sometimes be unpredictable, but he wouldn't have it any other way.

They needed time to talk, time to work through their feelings, but this was not the place. That only left one course of action left. Dare he risk it?

His contemplation was instantaneous. Of course he would. She would respect nothing less. Joshua's voice came out low, dangerous in tone. "I should have known. Two antics in one night."

Kit tossed her head and said nothing. She had to stand firm. Stand firm for her pride. Joshua's lips curled upward slightly, in a smile reminiscent of Rhett Butler before he stormed up the stairs carrying Scarlett. She froze as Joshua stepped forward. What was mere seconds seemed to take an eternity.

''Let's give them an antic to really write home about, shall we, Kit?'' Kit, rooted by his words was unable to move. He approached her, tossed her like a sack of flour over his shoulder and carried her toward the exit.

Chapter Fourteen

"Put me down!" Somehow Kit managed to find her voice. "Put me down, Joshua Parker, or I'll..."

"You'll do nothing."

Kit rained a few blows on his back with her fists, but Joshua just gently pinched her leg.

"Ow!" she yelled, more annoyed than hurt. She gave up pummeling him and instead kicked her legs.

"Hold still," he said, twisting her a little. "There's a photographer coming. We need to give them a good shot, and preferably not just of your derriere, cute as it is. I want us to go out in style."

Kit saw the flashbulbs go off. Oh, no. She had to get someone to stop him. People stared at her with astounded faces. Some snickered. And Cameron. Her brother was laughing and...taking pictures! He had a disposable camera and he was snapping away. She would kill him once she got free.

"Cameron!" She yelled across the room, it dawning that somehow her brother was in on all this. "Tell him to put me down! Do something!"

Cameron hunched his shoulders in laughter and

waved goodbye at her. "Remember what Father said. Be sensible, Kit."

"Cameron!" Kit shrieked, still being borne aloft through the ballroom. Her last view of her brother was of him taking out his cell phone and dialing.

Joshua dumped her down at the coat check. Kit made a move to bolt, but his voice stopped her. "Don't even think about it, Kit. Get your coat. We're going to talk, this time without an audience and without antics." He handed the coat-check girl his ticket. "I'll meet you right back here. If I were you I'd be here." With that he walked off.

Kit stared after him. Who did he think he was? There was no way she would just stand here and wait for him, not after the way he'd just treated her. She'd obeyed after that time at the casino, but this time she was sober and she refused. Kit handed the girl her ticket, the girl retrieved her fake fur.

"Cute guy," she remarked as Kit dropped money into the tip jar.

Kit turned and smiled. "Isn't he? Tell him I went to the ladies' room and I'll meet him right back here."

"Sure thing."

Kit smiled as she buttoned up the coat and walked away. That should give her a few minutes. She took the escalator to the lobby floor in order to avoid being caught waiting for an elevator.

Despite the cold, bitter wind slapping her face as she exited the hotel, Kit found her first bit of luck all night. Expecting to have to hail a cab, somehow her limo was miraculously pulling up to the curb. The heck with Cameron. After his failure to save her, her brother could be the one taking a cab home.

The uniformed doorman adjusted his scarf to block out the cold. "That's my limo." Kit told him as the wind tore at her hair and her heart. She looked around behind her once. No sign of Joshua.

Kit bent her head down to shield herself from the bitter gusts and to hide the tears that threatened to rain down her cheeks. In just a few seconds the nightmare would be over. The doorman waited to assist her with the limousine door.

The limo stopped, and a black gloved hand opened the door for her. Bending to duck another icy blast, Kit mumbled vague thanks and climbed in. She moved toward the middle of the seat, the ill wind already sucking the heat from the passenger area.

What was holding that doorman up? Why wasn't the door closing? The doorman must have gotten distracted. With a groan of disgust Kit scooted back over to reach for the door handle. Instead of connecting with the handle, she connected sharply with a black wool duster-covered bulk that was now entering her limo uninvited. The black bulk seemed to back in, and as the door closed Kit panicked.

Her driver, oblivious to the turmoil in back, quickly pulled away, and as a piece of black fabric flew into her hands Kit shrieked and thrust it away from her. As it hit the floor she realized it was her black dress.

"READY TO HAVE that talk now?"

Kit shrank back against the other side of the limo

as Joshua removed his black gloves and scratched an itch on the top of his left hand. He seemed so calm, as if he had been expecting her to bolt.

"I have nothing to say to you! Get out of my limo!" Kit picked up the phone and dialed Lyle. After a few seconds she slammed the unanswered unit down and pressed the privacy glass button several times to no avail. The glass remained up.

"What's going on?" Kit's voice rose an octave. "This is against the law. You can't do this to me!" In the midst of her tirade she paused, stricken. "Is that even Lyle up there?"

Joshua laughed, his deep voice filling the confines of the back of the limo. "It's Lyle. He's just under strict orders."

"Whose orders?" Kit snapped furiously. "He doesn't answer to you! It doesn't matter if you paid ten thousand or ten million for me! That doesn't give you the right to assume that you can order my driver around."

"I didn't. Your brother told Lyle not to let you out until I said you were being sensible."

Kit's shoulders slumped as the fight left her. A strange calm overtook her. "Set up again," she mumbled. "You commandeered my brother."

Joshua chuckled, and in the darkness the effect was positively breathtaking. "Actually Mark and Donna started it. They've known Cameron socially for years, and all four of us planned this, once we learned you weren't really engaged to Blaine Rourke."

Somehow they were now in the eye of the storm, Kit thought. The anger had subsided, and it would be useless to tell anything but the truth. "No. I'm not engaged to Blaine. I just stopped denying it after my father's heart attack. It made the press go away."

Joshua ran a hand through his hair. Passing street-lights caused the reddish highlights to shimmer. "That's what I learned. Cameron told me why you haven't been out anywhere."

"You've been meeting with my brother!"

"I have," he admitted. "You'll find we get along well. Anyway, Cameron insisted you weren't ready to see anyone."

"I haven't felt much like socializing." Kit pressed her head back against the smooth leather seat. She gazed out at the New York streetscape, trying to assess where she was. It was easy to figure out that Lyle was driving through Midtown, but where she was with Joshua was a complete blank. Her heart knew it hadn't stopped loving him. Jealousy had raged through her like a green flame when she had seen him in the clippings with another woman.

"Kit." Joshua's voice called her back from her thoughts. "Kit, we need to talk."

"Don't worry, I'm not pregnant."

"Kit." Joshua's use of her name coaxed her softly, defusing residual anger. "There are some things I need to say, things I never got to say because our visit to the farm got interrupted." Brown eyes flecked with gold focused on hers. God, Kit thought, he was beautiful. She could no longer fault his fans, or whoever else threw themselves at him.

Her voice sounded far away. "Joshua, there's nothing else to say that you didn't that day. You were right. What we had was a mistake. Some cruise magic." Kit saw the surprise and hurt come into those brown pools. Her lip quivered.

"Kit, I was angry. I felt betrayed. Then, the longer I thought about it, the more I knew that you wouldn't deliberately destroy someone to get ahead, *ma chérie.*"

"No," she whispered. "I wouldn't."

"I know. I was wrong. I didn't listen to you or give you a chance. Because of my past history with Marilyn and the articles she wrote, I judged you guilty of betrayal. I thought you were going to rehash everything my father and I had finally put behind us."

"No, I'd only kept the clippings because I had these visions of Marilyn paying the maid for my trash. There never was a safe time or place to shred them."

"When I saw you burned them I knew I was wrong about you, but by then you were long gone with Blaine."

"Oh." Kit stared at him.

"I let my prejudices of the past influence me, and I'm sorry. I hurt you, and all because of my pride. You see, I've always disappointed my father. First I sided with my mother, never realizing that their divorce was a two-way street, and that my parents had drifted apart. Neither of them was to blame, but I didn't realize that until much later. Instead I blamed my father and hated the summers my sisters and I had to spend with him.

"I lashed out constantly, even going so far as to tell him that if he hadn't been so busy saving Quebec and the Canadian federation, he could have saved his marriage."

In the darkness of the limo Kit instinctively reached out with her right hand and put it over his. From his admission, she knew Joshua trusted her. The warmth of his skin burned under hers.

"Anyway, I did flunk one of my college courses, which enraged my father because the professor was a close personal friend of his. My father was more embarrassed than anything, especially because, at the time, he was up for a Senate appointment, and I was running my mouth off in the press about how horrid he was."

He shifted, and Kit withdrew her hand. "Press scares me, Kit. My relationship with my father is too precarious to take lightly. But after you left, I realized something else. My relationship with you is too precious to throw away."

Kit's resolve shattered at his words. She loved this man, but she couldn't let him know. Her mind agonized, but she knew she couldn't handle the pain of loving and losing him again. "Please don't put me through this. I can't handle another affair with you again."

"An affair?" Joshua barely contained his fury as the words flew out between gritted teeth. "That's all you thought it was? No wonder your brother told me to tell you to be sensible.''

"Of course. What else could you call what happened between us?'' Kit's voice wavered, her thoughts thrown again by that *sensible* word.

Silence settled in the limo for a long moment before Joshua finally spoke. ''Perhaps it's called love?''

"Humph.'' Kit snorted, her stomach fluttering. How she wanted to believe him! She eyed him suspiciously. From the tone of his voice she thought he told the truth. In the dim light she could see that he even appeared haggard, with lines on his face that weren't there before.

"Oh, Kit. How can you question that I love you? I let you throw water all over me, and toted you out in the most ungracious way possible. Everyone in the city will see that picture tomorrow morning, and if not, your brother took some to show your father.''

Hope filled her. ''You were pretty outrageous.''

"But it worked,'' he said.

"It worked,'' she admitted with a smile. ''You outmaneuvered me with your own antic.''

He leaned forward and traced her cheekbone with his finger. ''I had to risk it. You have a fiery Irish temper, darling, and I knew you wouldn't stay at the coat check. But we needed to talk. I needed to tell you how I felt.''

"Cameron called the limo when you carried me out,'' Kit said, a dazzling joy beginning to spread through her.

"Of course he did. You're such a darling. Don't

you know you've captured my heart in a way no other woman has ever come close to doing?"

Belief spread across Kit's face, and Joshua reached forward to take her hands. Slowly he inched closer to her, his leg daring to press against her thigh. Sincerity radiated from him, and she basked in it.

"Kit, I love you. I want to spend the rest of my life with you. I want to marry you and whisk you off into the sunset. You've dominated my thoughts, my heart, my soul."

Joshua lowered his lips and kissed her forehead briefly. "It's been hell without you, Kit. Worse, after I met with Cameron, he insisted I follow his rules. He wanted to wait for your father to recuperate and for you both to make amends. Having little choice except to just barge in on you, I agreed. Then you failed to show up anywhere. Tonight was my last hope."

Kit rubbed her fingers together. The back of the limo had definitely gotten warm. "Joshua, I've been a fool. I'm sorry."

"I was a fool, too." He lifted her palm and pressed his lips to it. "But that makes us equal. And we are equal, my darling. Equally matched, equally in love and equal in spirit."

He silenced her answer with a long kiss, his lips reigniting the smoldering fire between them. Slowly he lifted his head from her mouth and gazed at her again, as if seeing her for the first time.

"Kit, you have captured a part of me that I wasn't

ever going to let anyone possess. I belong to you, *ma belle.*"

A small tear began to cascade down Kit's cheek. He did love her. "Kit, darling, don't cry." Joshua reached up to touch her tears. "What is it?"

"I almost didn't come tonight"

"I had decided to storm your castle tomorrow if you didn't show. Cameron even told me I could, that your father had approved if tonight failed."

In one moment Kit realized how lucky she really was. "My father will adore you. We had long, wonderful talks, and I told him about us. I think I'm finally getting some Irish luck. He said I can write more serious stories and use my own name. But the best part is that you love me."

"I do."

"And I do love you, Joshua." Her voice was low and husky.

"Then marry me, Kit O'Brien. Marry me and be my wife."

Kit captured his hands and felt the strength and warmth that radiated from his palms. "I'm accepting your proposal, Joshua. Yes, I'll marry you. I've loved you since that first kiss, probably even before. But, I'm warning you, I'm not going to be a pushover, no matter how much you paid for me, no matter how well everyone can conspire against me, and no matter how many he-man antics you pull to keep me grounded."

Joshua laughed and traced her lips with his forefinger. "Ah, well then, you'll have to keep your end of the bargain."

"What's that?"

"Just be my wife." As they passed under a street-light, Kit saw a glittering diamond ring in Joshua's palm.

The implication of the jewelry her father had insisted she wear was now clear. Joshua slid the ring on her finger, and Kit quivered from the intimacy of it.

"You know, my love, I'm looking forward to getting to know Cameron and your father. And my family is dying to meet you. They'll give us maybe a few days of peace before they'll clamor to find out what happened between us tonight. Everyone at the table was related to me."

He threaded a hand through her silken hair and began to stroke the back of her neck. He kissed her neck, his lips moving up to her ears to kiss the fiery ice jewelry adorning the edges. Kit trembled as the sensation caressed through her body, and she stretched to press her body fully against his. The movement did little to satisfy her overwhelming desire for the man that she loved with a burning fervor.

Kit began to play with a button on Joshua's coat. "Am I being sensible now?"

"I would say you are." Joshua answered, his voice husky.

"Good." Kit reached forward and knocked on the privacy glass twice. Her sudden movement caught Joshua off guard, and they tumbled to the spacious floor as the limousine sped up and switched lanes. Within moments the limo dipped into the Queens Midtown Tunnel and under the East River.

In the artificial lights of the tunnel Joshua wrapped his arms around Kit. "Queens?"

"Long Island. Summerset House." Kit grinned slyly as she traced his chin with her forefinger. "Don't tell me Cameron didn't explain his knocking system."

Joshua gave a chuckle. "He did. I'm just surprised you know about it."

"Well, just because I've never needed to use his playboy tactics doesn't mean I don't know about them. Let that be a lesson to you. We are equal." Kit slid her fingers into his bow tie and began to undo the knot.

"How can I argue with that?"

"Flattery will get you everywhere."

"Good. I'm counting on it."

Kit's newly adorned finger slid under Joshua's coat, and she tugged at his shirt buttons. Catching her movement, Joshua gave a low groan and lowered his mouth to hers.

"I've been without you for far too long, my love," he murmured, his lips urgent and demanding. Instantly Kit responded to the man she loved, kissing him back with an ardor freshly released.

"Your dress is evil," he said planting kisses all down the side of her throat until he reached her neckline. "It's been driving me crazy all night. I didn't think any dress could be worse than your black one, but this dress is *très séduisante*. Very seductive, *ma belle*. And don't worry, when I use my native language I'll make sure you know what it means. I never want you to feel left out.''

As the limo exited the tunnel, night again enveloped them. Kit's earrings glittered like stars as she lowered her lips and slowly kissed the man she was going to marry. She lifted her head and smiled.

''I'm behaving very sensibly now, don't you think?''

''So much that you're driving me absolutely insane. I love you, Kit.''

''Good, because I love you and I've been very, very lonely. I'm never going to let you go. So, have you ever made love in a limo?''

''Are you propositioning me?''

''And if I am?'' she parried easily, her smooth skin on fire.

''Then we'll join the limo club together.'' He kissed her bare flesh, and he groaned with anticipation of loving the woman who owned his heart and possessed his soul. ''How much time do we have?''

''Forever.'' She recaptured Joshua's lips with her own and gave him a long, deep kiss that sent his head spinning.

''Kit!'' Joshua's one word said it all.

''I'm serious,'' she told him. ''Lyle will drive around Long Island all night if necessary.''

In one fluid movement she lowered her body to meet his. Sparks flew, and the diamonds sparkled like wishing stars.

''Wanting to turn in the driveway is three knocks.''

Epilogue

The *Tattler*, Saturday, February 15
Joelle's Around the Town
Heiress Ties the Knot

In a lavish ceremony at the Church of St. Thomas More, Kit O'Brien and Joshua Parker married yesterday. The bride wore a white original Viscountie gown (one can only speculate on the cost of that) and her matron of honor was Eleni Jacobs, *Scene* executive editor. Joshua's sisters and brothers served in the wedding party, as did Kit's brother, New York City's most eligible bachelor, Cameron O'Brien. Guests at the wedding at the exquisite Waldorf Astoria reception included Mayor Rogers, Governor Gladstone, and Vice President Mel Baker, several media moguls and noted dignitaries and even Kit's cruise roommates. Family members in attendance included Joshua's father, the Honorable Gasper de Bettencourt of Quebec, and Joshua's mother, travel guide author Angelina

Cooper, and her husband, Dave Cooper. Michael O'Brien, patriarch of O'Brien Publications, is said to be delighted with the match and can't wait until his first grandchild arrives. No, you heard the truth here—Kit's not pregnant. Yet. I promise to keep you posted. The happy couple plans to divide their time between Upstate New York and Oyster Bay, Long Island, after a nice long honeymoon in Paradise.

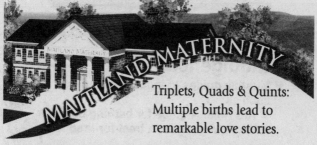

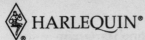

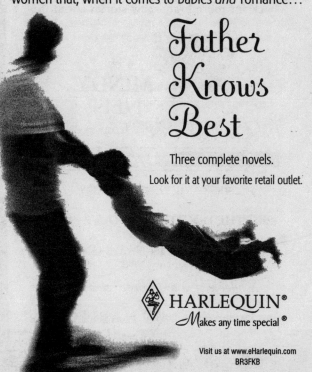

What a baby wants...
a baby gets!

Mommy and Me

From bestselling author

MURIEL JENSEN

The magic and delight of parenthood shine through in these three full-length novels of babies turned matchmakers!

Available in December 2001 at your favorite retail outlet.

HARLEQUIN®

Makes any time special ®

WITH HARLEQUIN AND SILHOUETTE

There's a romance to fit your every mood.

Passion

Harlequin Temptation

Harlequin Presents

Silhouette Desire

Pure Romance

Harlequin Romance

Silhouette Romance

Home & Family

Harlequin
American Romance

Silhouette
Special Edition

A Longer Story With More

Harlequin
Superromance

Suspense & Adventure

Harlequin Intrigue

Silhouette Intimate
Moments

Humor

Harlequin Duets

Historical

Harlequin Historicals

Special Releases

Other great
romances
to explore

*H*ugh Blake,
soon to become stepfather to
the Maitland clan, has produced three
high-performing offspring of his own. But
at the rate they're going, they're never going to
make him a grandpa!

There's *Suzanne*, a work-obsessed CEO whose Christmas spirit could use a little topping up....

And *Thomas*, a lawyer whose ability to hold on to the woman he loves is evaporating by the minute....

And *Diane*, a teacher so dedicated to her teenage students she hasn't noticed she's put her own life on hold.

But there's a Christmas wake-up call in store
for the Blake siblings. Love *and* Christmas miracles
are in store for all three!

Maitland Maternity Christmas

A collection from three of Harlequin's favorite authors

Muriel Jensen
Judy Christenberry
& Tina Leonard

Look for it in November 2001.